Ans	M.L.
ASH	MLW
Bev	Mt.Pl
C.C.	NLM
C.P.	Ott
Dick	PC
DRZ	PH
ECH	P.P.
ECS	Pion.P.
Gar	Q.A.
GRM	Riv
GSP	RPP
G.V.	Ross
Har	S.C.
JPCP	St.A.
KEN	St.J
K.L.	St.Joa
K.M.	St.M.
L.H.	Sgt
LO	T.H.
Lyn	TLLO
L.V.	T.M.
McC	T.T.
McG	Ven
McQ	Vets
MIL	VP
	Wat
	Wed
	WIL
	W.L.

PAY BACK

Rick Manton and Thelma Wain were two young people in love — but they were also grifters, who recognised no moral code and considered themselves above the law. And when mobster Dan Sweder moved to take over the drug traffic in Los Angeles, they found their own small dope dealing operation was being squeezed out. Rick and Thelma had only one answer: Dan Sweder had to die! So they set out to 'eliminate' him — two small-time crooks against the Mob!

NORMAN LAZENBY

PAY BACK

Complete and Unabridged

LINFORD
Leicester

First published in Great Britain

First Linford Edition
published 2009

British Library CIP Data

Lazenby, Norman A. (Norman Austin)
    Pay back- -(Linford mystery library)
    1. Swindlers and swindling- -Fiction.
    2. Gangsters- -Fiction.
    3. Drug dealers- -Fiction.
    4. Los Angeles (Calif.)- -Fiction.
    5. Suspense fiction. 6. Large type books.
    I. Title II Series
    813.5′4–dc22

    ISBN 978–1–84782–753–1

Published by
F. A. Thorpe (Publishing)
Anstey, Leicestershire

Set by Words & Graphics Ltd.
Anstey, Leicestershire
Printed and bound in Great Britain by
T. J. International Ltd., Padstow, Cornwall

This book is printed on acid-free paper

1

Target for Death

Rick Manton lowered the .38 Spanish automatic; stared through the grimy window. The traffic honked and crawled in the concrete chasm below. He looked grimly at the wide window directly opposite him on the other side of the road, and thought the range was plenty for a small heater. Maybe he ought to get a rifle!

Sweder had moved away from his window, anyhow. The lean, in-bitten swine had moved just as Rick Manton's finger had started to curve.

Rick slid back across the empty, dusty office. He stuck the gun in his shoulder holster. He buttoned his jacket, revealing his slim waist and wide shoulders. He picked his hat off a peg behind the door; slanted it over thick black hair. With a faint grin on his good-looking, but

1

nevertheless taut, poker face, he went out of the unused office.

The top part of the old block was devoid of tenants. There was no elevator; he went down the stairs swiftly; reached the street. He walked along, mingling with the crowds, and thought Los Angeles was a jungle, a cement jungle.

His auto was standing in a parking zone only fifty yards away. He had figured fifty yards was enough considering the idea he had in mind. He got in and drove down Pico, which ran from the beach at Santa Monica right into the heart of L.A.

Rick Manton rolled his Oldsmobile into the parking lot of a trailer camp some ten minutes later. He got out, slammed the auto door and walked along until he reached a big green trailer. It was big enough to be a home, and was sited on a permanent pitch with electricity and water and a small garden plot ornamenting the front.

The door opened to his double rap, and he went inside. He sat on the settee and grinned at the red-haired girl in the revealing dress.

'I could do with a rifle, baby. Guess it'll be easy. I'll have to get me a long heater.'

'You saw him?' Thelma Wain leaned forward, and Rick instinctively dropped his dark eyes.

'Sure. I saw him, Dan Sweder, the big business tycoon! He'll stand at that window of his once too often! Just let me get a rifle.'

'You could get him in the street — at his house — anywhere!' Her red lips were parted in an eager smile.

'It's the getaway, sugar. Yeah, I got it figured! With a long heater, I can get him neat, get outa that building fast, walk to the auto and drive away.'

'Payoff for Mister Dan Sweder,' she said viciously, her green eyes blazing.

'Yeah. Well, I'll see about getting the rifle but first — ' He pulled her down on to the settee; cushioned his lips brutally against her red ones. He held her in a tight embrace. She wriggled, and slipped free with an excited laugh.

'Say, people can see into this trailer! Wipe your lips, big boy!'

Silk handkerchief to his mouth, he

retorted: 'Save your pep until I get back, kid. I gotta see about that long heater.'

He went out to his auto and drove away, reaching downtown Los Angeles some fifteen minutes later. He went into a third-rate poolroom, strode past the assortment of punks and hoodlums using the tables and made for a small office at the back.

Some time later Rick Manton returned to his car carrying something that looked like a battered golf-club bag. As a matter of cockeyed fact, it was. And inside was a good rifle with a telescopic sights attachment.

Grimly satisfied, he drove away and returned to the trailer park on the corner of Pico and Centinela Avenue. He left the battered golf bag in his auto. He went into the trailer, grinning at the sight of Thelma's face at one of the windows.

Over on Pico Boulevard, Dan Sweder paced his office floor and did not realise how near he was to death. He knew he had enemies. He did not think any one of them had gotten around to plotting his death. He lived hard, and wasn't prone to fears.

He thought he was successful and usually he put the fear of God into other people.

The man sitting indolently in a chromium tubular easy-chair opposite Dan Sweder's desk was a smooth-faced product of L.A. streets and a materialistic civilisation. He was mean, black-eyed, swift-thinking, but with little more education than a chimpanzee.

'Look, Zac, you know this is important! Get down to the yacht at Santa Monica. Wait for me there. I got some things to do. Hell, I never get any peace! You'd think a guy could get peace if he has dough! All I get is more grief!'

'That's because you hand it out to guys who get in your way,' said Zac Ortmann. 'Oke, I'll go down.'

'Yeah, and keep that twisty shamus talking until I get down. I got things to say to a guy who takes my dough and then tries to chisel!'

Zac Ortmann got up lithely. 'I'd use slugs on any private richard who crossed me, but you're the boss.'

'No slugs! Just keep Napier waiting on the yacht.'

'Sure, boss, sure!' said the other smoothly, and went out of the office.

Dan Sweder's lean face stared across his desk at the photograph of a woman. After a moment, he reached out and brought the framed portrait closer to him. He studied the woman's dark, flaunting beauty. He smiled sombrely, then put the photograph down again. He lit a cigarette thoughtfully. He was thinking that Gloria Grahame was all woman and the only trouble was she attracted too many other guys.

He got up and walked slowly across to the wide window that graced the side of his office, and looked down into Pico. Thoughtfully, he stared at the automobiles, the yellow cabs, the sidewalks filled with well-dressed passers-by. Staring out of the window was a habit with him. It didn't mean anything.

He went to his phone, put his hand on the instrument and paused. Then with a shrug he moved away. He figured he would go out instead.

A few minutes later, he had taken a sedan out of a garage in a nearby alley.

He drove down Pico, turned at an intersection; went up Sepulveda Boulevard for two miles. He reached the rural neighbourhoods of Brentwood Park; passed some big, newly erected houses perched on landscaped lots that still looked a bit raw.

Half a mile of this and he rolled the auto swiftly up a driveway and halted in front of a ranch-type house. He knew his way around. He walked into the house, swift strides taking him into a lounge that was empty except for the deep carpet that dulled his footsteps, floral-covered chairs, an electric organ, flowers in vases and small tables.

Dan Sweder stabbed a finger to a bell; waited. He looked a lean, hard, medium-sized figure in his striped tropical suit.

A white-jacketed Japanese servant came into the room and smiled at Dan Sweder.

'Where is Miss Grahame?' he jerked.

'She is in the house or the grounds somewhere. Shall I find her for you, sir?'

'Never mind,' growled the other. 'I'd — I'd — like to surprise her!'

He walked out of the room; went along a wide passage decorated with cream enamel. He opened a door and looked into a patio enclosed on three sides by the shape of the house. There were three reclining chairs and a table, and Gloria Grahame occupied one of the chairs. She smiled up to him, her eyes large, dark liquid pools.

'Hello, Dan. What brings you here?'

His face cracked in a smile. 'I guess it was you.' He looked around, halting his eyes suspiciously on the ashtray on the table. He eased across, fingered the cigarette stubs. Only one or two had lipstick traces. He glanced at Gloria. 'There's been a guy here,' he said harshly.

She rose gracefully, her green dress falling nicely against full thighs. The dress gave her the usual sexy, Hollywood lines.

'You're crazy!' she stated, her full lips pouting. 'You're as jealous as hell. Always it is the same — you think there's been a guy around if you see a cigarette butt that doesn't belong to me. Gawd knows what will happen the day you find a cigar or a guy's hat!'

An unpleasant twist came to Dan Sweder's lip. His hands cupped slowly.

He didn't know it, but he was strangling thin air.

'Don't let that happen, baby!'

She laughed; red lips against a flawless creamy skin. 'Look, Dan, I'm resting. I've got my TV show to do this afternoon at PDK — as you know. I've been rehearsing new tunes on that damned electric organ all morning. It's work, Dan, and I'm tired! Come and sit down beside me and forget your jealousy.'

He didn't wait until they sat down; he grabbed her and kissed her almost brutally, as if he was a man who had been up in the mountains out of sight of women for years. He was always like that with Gloria Grahame.

After the kiss — 'You're right, I am crazy — about you! Always I think there's another guy! It crawls into my mind, honey, and I can't stop it. I get to thinking there's a guy making passes, or a guy holding your hand. Only time I know there ain't is when you're with me!'

'Oh, you fool, it's just you and me, Dan!' She breathed the words against his lips.

They did sit down, in the same seat. There was plenty of room because Gloria's slim form was pressed right against Dan Sweder. She played him along, discouraging him here and encouraging him there. She thought she was in love with him, but she wasn't sure. How could anybody be sure about love, anyway?

After a while, he returned to staring at the cigarette butts. They drew his attention as if they exerted some sullen fascination. He knew they were not her brand.

She suddenly spoke edgily. 'Why don't you quiz the servant, Dan? I'm sure he would help you — for a suitable tip!'

He looked sour, unhappy. 'Aw, hell. I'm a crazy, jealous guy!'

'Well, snap out of it. I'll tell you when there's another guy. How's business? You still going to buy me that bracelet?'

'Sure, honey, sure.' He grinned, kissed her passionately.

Then: 'Business is okay, I guess. There's mazuma from the gambling parties on the yacht down at Santa Monica, and the office is a good base for my other racket.'

Gloria wasn't crooked. She got high pay for her TV programmes of popular music on the electric organ. But she knew Dan Sweder was head guy in a dope purveying organization, and that the work was done from his offices. It was like a legitimate business. Nothing came into the office except letters in code and other strange forms, telephone calls and cunning guys calling for instructions. There wasn't a packet of dope within a mile of the building. Dan never looked at the stuff, and wouldn't employ a dopey for a million bucks.

'I'll come down to your yacht tonight,' she promised. 'I like the yacht. Gee, how much money does one have to earn to buy yachts? My programme is doing fine, but I'm nowhere near that sorta money. And I can't win on your tables, Dan!'

'Be good to me and I'll have one fixed — but maybe you'd clean me out!'

He left her warm arms reluctantly. He had to get down to Santa Monica to see Zac Ortmann and the twisty shamus, Walt Napier.

He got into the sedan and drove away, arriving at the yacht harbour at Santa Monica some twenty minutes later, having used the fast, new freeways. His yacht was a neat vessel lying at a pier. Brass, white paint and mahogany gleamed at him as he stepped on board. He went down below; found Zac Ortmann and Walt Napier waiting in a little lounge.

Dan Sweder handed cigarettes around. He dragged on his own when it was alight. Then he leaned across the table and grabbed Walt Napier's arm, pulled the man hard against the wood.

'You took my dough! I wanted to know who the hell was seeing Miss Grahame the nights she didn't come to this yacht! And what did you do? You crossed me!'

Walt Napier was forty-eight years old. He had been a private detective so long he couldn't think straight because of the twisty things he had seen. He liked to slink past trouble like some mongrel in a gutter avoiding a kick.

'Look, Dan, I didn't cross you!' he exclaimed huskily. 'I just couldn't get the information!'

Dan Sweder raised his hand threateningly.

'Like hell! You were paid to keep quiet! You twisted on me! Don't tell me you couldn't get information! You could snoop in and out of Fort Knox! Now give, chiseller! What sorta flaming news you got about Gloria Grahame?'

2

Rick Attacks

About ninety minutes later, long after Walt Napier had departed for a drink, white-faced and shaken, Dan Sweder and Zac Ortmann were walking slowly along the sidewalk of a swank development in Beverly Hills. Dan's sedan was at the curb. They didn't walk far from the auto. They turned, stared around, mostly for sign of a cop. Then Dan tapped his young thug on the arm. 'C'mon!'

They walked up the driveway, avoided the main door. They followed the patio around the house. They were lucky. They found their man sitting in a wicker chair, drinking, dressed comfortably in shorts and open-neck shirt.

'You're Rex Rand!' grated Dan Sweder, and he leaned forward menacingly.

The man was good-looking, mature and definitely in his forties. His startled blue eyes searched Dan Sweder.

'I don't know you — ' he began.

'All the better!' Sheer hatred thickened the other's voice. 'All right, Zac!'

Without another word, the two mobsters fell on Rex Rand. Zac Ortmann slammed a fist into Rand's face. Ringed fingers scraped skin away. Dan Sweder hacked a low punch into the man's ribs. Air seemed to gasp out of him. He half-rose but was sent sprawling by another blow. He was unable to shout for help. He just did not have the breath for that. The mobsters made no noise except the dull thuds as fists slammed into Rex Rand. Finally, they left him moaning and lying limply in his chair. Dan Sweder had only a few rasping words to say and they echoed in the unfortunate man's ears like a grim warning.

'Keep away from Gloria Grahame, sucker! Get even within sight of her again and you'll be a dead guy!'

Dan Sweder and Zac Ortmann walked swiftly to the waiting auto, piled in and drove away. Before Rex Rand even got the courage to phone the police, the two gangsters were miles away.

Rex Rand gave his account of the outrage to the cops, and then phoned his doctor. The handsome actor was worried about his face. Judging by the punishment he had taken, the doctor would have to be good to get his appearance quickly back to normal.

Long after the cops had slashed up and got his account of the two hoods who had attacked him, and after the doctor had worked on his face, Rex Rand got around to phoning Gloria Grahame.

The man had some guts; he was an actor but no pansy. Also he thought Gloria Grahame was the tops, and he had ambitions concerning her. He thought he would phone Gloria and tell her how he had fought off two gorillas who had warned him to steer clear of her in future.

He gave her the account, embellished a bit. She was worried at once.

'Oh, my Gawd! He might have killed you!'

He was puzzled. 'Look, honey, who were those guys? What was the idea of mussing me up? Why did they set on me?

16

They told me to keep away from you! I don't get it. Do you know them, honey?'

'I — I guess not!'

'But you said something about how he might have killed me!'

'I — I — was thinking of a man who is crazy about me. I've had to avoid this man. He's — he's dangerous! I — I — '

'What's this guy's name? Is he a mean, hard guy?'

'I'd better not say,' gasped Gloria Grahame. 'I'm probably making a mistake. You'd better take care, Rex!'

'The cops have been here,' he growled, 'but all I could give them was a description that might fit a lot of guys.'

'Now, look, Rex,' she said desperately. 'You'd better not see me for some time. I'm — I'm worried about you. Maybe it's this crazy guy — and he might kill you! We'd better play it safe. Don't try to see me for the next few days. For your own sake, Rex.'

'You sound very confused — even scared. Why shouldn't I see you? I'm in love with you, Gloria! These hoods can't scare me!'

As he spoke into the phone, his split lips pained him and he grimaced.

'You mustn't try to see me,' Gloria insisted. 'Keep away from this house.'

He considered. Then: 'Well, maybe I can phone you? Maybe you're right. Maybe I ought to play it safe. These guys must be nuts.'

'Okay, you can phone me, Rex.'

'Fine. 'Bye, baby! And take care of yourself, My God, if I thought you were in danger, I'd be over right away!'

'I'm not in danger. You mustn't come over here! Now please play it safe — after all, it will be only a few days of separation, maybe.'

'All right. And, honey, I'm crazy about you.'

Her voice cooed in the receiver. 'You know how I feel about you, darling. Now take care of yourself.'

With that Rex Rand had to be satisfied. But he was puzzled, and, to be truthful, he was suspicious. He was not a teenager in love. He had been in love before, and was wised up to the amazing tricks women can play with their men. There was a lot he didn't understand. And although he had sounded off over the phone, he figured maybe he should play for safety and keep away from Gloria Grahame for a little while.

A bit later a newspaperman rang him and got a few lines from him. The result was by evening the *L.A. Star* carried a front-page account of the assault, with a photograph of Rex Rand. No names were mentioned because nobody had the names of the hoods. The story was the usual protest against gangsterism in the fair city of El Pueblo de Nuestra Senora, la Reina de los Angeles — commonly known as L.A.

Walt Napier, the shamus, sitting in his office on Sunset Boulevard, read the account and paled.

Dan Sweder, smoking a cigar, reclining on a settee in his yacht at Santa Monica, read the paragraphs with a sour smile. Then he flung the paper away. There was work to do because there was to be a gambling session that night on the yacht.

Rick Manton was with Thelma Wain in her trailer. Rick had a room in downtown

Los Angeles, but he wasn't there much now that he and Thelma were so pally. Rick read the newspaper account and wondered idly which bunch of L.A. hoods had beaten up the guy. But that was all. It wasn't very interesting. He turned to the racing section and wondered which of the fillies would win next day at Agua Caliente. Then after relaxing the mind with that, he put the sheet away and returned to the burning topic of the moment for Thelma and himself.

'Maybe I could get Dan Sweder better at his yacht down at Santa Monica. Maybe he'll be there tonight. I could get him with the rod and leave this damn long heater here. Sure is inconvenient to carry around!'

'You just get him, Rick!' snapped Thelma. 'When I think of the dirty deal we got from that louse I — I — '

'Sure, sure. Take it easy, kid. Best to figure this out. Don't burn yourself up over this guy. Maybe I'll go down to this yacht tonight after all.'

'I'll be with you!'

'Now, look — '

'I said I'll be with you! I'm in on this. When that slob dies, I'd like to be around. I'd like to see it happen. The way I feel, I don't want to just read about it in the papers!'

Rick smiled thinly: jerked a thumb and she came to him willingly. She nestled against him, her red hair fragrant in his face. They clung passionately to each other for a minute. They were always that way.

'Okay, we'll go down to the slob's yacht. Maybe I'll get him. I'd like to snatch some of the dough he has. Maybe that would hurt the swine more than a quick death.'

'He owes us dough.'

'You sure said it,' Rick muttered, 'He has forced us out of the dope business in L.A. One time we had some good contacts. We knew the suppliers and they knew us. We got our supplies of dope and were able to get around selling the stuff. Then Dan Sweder decides to corner the whole damned racket in L.A. We're out. We can't get supplies. We can't make a decent buck out of distributing dope because Dan Sweder has sewn the whole racket up. We ain't in business any more because we can't get anyone to deal with. Everybody is scared of that swine Dan Sweder!'

'All that's as good as owing us dough,' said Thelma angrily. 'Say, I think it's kinda disgraceful we can't get the chance to operate! If Dan Sweder was dead. his organization would fall to bits. We'd be able to move in; pick up our old contacts.'

'Sure, we've been around all this before, honey. Yeah, maybe it would be good if Dan Sweder wasn't around. But maybe we can get to that after we snatch some of his dough as recompense for business we've lost up-to-date.'

Her green eyes were speculative. 'Maybe you're right. Dough is nice. Then the long slide to hell for Mister Dan Sweder and back to our usual operating! Yeah, why not?'

His dark eyes searched hers eagerly. 'Yeah, why not?'

They went out that night when the neons were throwing a green and red flush over the centre of Los Angeles and the famous Sunset Strip was just a channel for a thousand automobiles carrying folks looking for a high old time on the entertainment hell-around.

There was no one to tell Rick Manton and Thelma Wain that they were two unscrupulous young people. They were just a guy and a gal with the background of a great city. Rick and Thelma thought they knew plenty. They thought they could get around and only flub-dubs bothered to examine consciences!

Rick parked his Oldsmobile on some wasteland near the entrance to the yacht club at Santa Monica. As the engine died, he stared through the windscreen at the dotting lights scattered over the harbour. The silken night lay lightly over the harbour. The piers were well-lighted. He saw the navigation lights of several large yachts.

'Okay, let's go.' He touched Thelma. 'Sure you won't stay?'

'I go with you, you big lug!'

'Affectionate!' He grinned. 'All right, I got the .38 Spanish rod — just in case we got to obliterate Mister Tycoon Dan

Sweder instead of lifting some of his dough.'

'You know his yacht?'

'Sure. Calls it *Green Lady*. Holds his gambling parties there — everybody knows that including some cops who've figured it's good business to leave Dan Sweder alone.'

They got out of the auto. They did not approach the gateway to the yacht club harbour. It was easy to climb over the low, white-painted rail and walk down the bank. If there was a gatekeeper, they did not want the man to notice them.

The yacht named *Green Lady* lay at the end of the west pier. They approached fairly close and then halted in the cover of a board holding two lifebelts. From this position they were able to watch the blaze of light on the *Green Lady*. While they were there, a party of folks got out of an auto further down the pier, where it was wide enough to turn a car, and walked up to the yacht. They went on board, were greeted by a man in a peaked cap who stood at the head of a narrow gateway.

'The suckers!' murmured Rick Manton.

'That ain't the way we'll get on the *Green Lady*!'

He hadn't any solid ideas about what he would do when he did get on the yacht. He wasn't the U.S. Army planning a battlefront. He was just a guy and he liked to hell along. He was usually lucky and he got results. Rick Manton never stopped to think there might be a time when he would be unlucky.

When the other party had disappeared down below the yacht's deck. Rick muttered to Thelma: 'Go along an' talk to that guy. Get him interested — you know what would interest him!'

'Yeah? And what will you be doing?'

'I'll be on that craft while you're talking, and I'll dispose of that gink. Just you watch!'

She nodded, and coolly sauntered along the pier. After progressing some yards, the man on the yacht turned his head to look at her.

Rick Manton waited. Very quickly Thelma was talking to the man. Rick heard him laugh. Seemed like Thelma had got him going! Rick slid away from the board. Crouching, he made for the side of the pier. He got to the iron ladder he'd noticed earlier and he went down a few rungs. Then he leaned forward; was able to grab at a rope trailing from the yacht. He hauled himself up, grinning with satisfaction. So far as he was concerned, it was as easy as that!

He cat-footed along the deck. He came up behind the man with the peaked cap. As Rick got his gun out of his shoulder rig, he thought the guy's peaked cap wasn't going to help him none!

The next second he sprang at the man, swinging the gun butt in a vicious arc. The gun connected with peaked cap and skull. The man dropped instantly, silently, like a lead weight suddenly released. He made a thud as he hit the deck planking. Rick thrust his gun into his rig, grabbed at the man. He heaved him up and went to the yacht's rail. For a second Rick Manton hesitated, and then, with a grim feeling, thrust the man into the harbour. The splash sounded dully. Thelma was at his side, her breathing a little excited.

'He had to go,' snapped Rick. 'If I left him somewhere, he'd waken up in no time and yell like blazes. C'mon, we're snooping down below!'

3

Robbery with Violence

Dan Sweder watched the play for some time. His lean face broke into a few lines of satisfaction. The small stateroom was warm and acrid with smoke and people. A loud hubbub filled the room, with the accompaniment of the roulette wheel and the snap of cards. A waiter, immaculate in evening dress, set up the drinks for the customers. It was all profit and Dan liked any gimmick that made a profit. Maybe this wasn't as big as the dope game, but it was interesting. More than once he had toyed with the idea of setting up another boat, perhaps in another harbour down the coast.

Zac Ortmann was playing poker with some other men and trying to add to his income. He was really on hand in case something rough jagged up and a hustler was needed.

Dan Sweder walked nonchalantly to where Gloria Grahame played the wheel. She was having fair luck. The wheel wasn't rigged that night. Dan believed in allowing the customers some pleasures. Some of them had to win so that they could bring their pals in — usually on a night when the wheel had a special little adjustment!

'I like to see you getting the luck, baby!' he whispered in her ear.

'But I'd like to win more! How much have I to win to buy a yacht like this?'

Her voice was music in his ears. He burned for her.

'You could regard the yacht as yours,' he said carelessly.

'Really?'

'Yeah. Sure. You know how I feel about you. Anything I've got is yours.'

'Oh, like that!' She laughed enticingly. 'I thought for a moment you were going to hand me the papers!'

'Say, let's go to my cabin — to talk!' he said, and he didn't mean talking at all.

'Okay, Dan. I think I've played long enough, anyway.'

She rose and together they walked from the stateroom. Their absence was not noticed, except by Zac Ortmann, and he grinned cynically.

Dan Sweder escorted Gloria Grahame to his cabin. The door clicked carelessly behind them. He went to a buffet and poured some drinks. Bringing the glasses to her, he said, 'Pity you and me got to work so hard. Gee, we never get any fun. You with that TV show every afternoon and me with my racket and this yacht most nights! Why, we oughta get to hell out of it, go somewhere on this yacht, have some fun!'

'Separate rooms?' she inquired archly.

He grinned. 'Anything you like. I got keys to all of 'em!'

She was playing him along, and he was taking it. But Walt Napier had told him certain things about Rex Rand. Dan Sweder knew she had been playing a double game. That would stop. Rex Rand would slide out of the picture if he was smart.

Dan Sweder did not intend to challenge her about Rex Rand. He knew he had to be careful how he played a dame like Gloria. She wasn't some cheap floosie, glad of a guy with mazuma. Gloria had class. She had intelligence and talent as well as looks. She was well-known on TV screens. All that meant she had to be played along.

Dan Sweder had choked back his jealousy, and had been helped by the fact that Rex Rand had been a nice victim. He'd worked out a lot of anger on him.

As to Gloria, she knew just how dangerous Dan Sweder could be. But he had money. Admittedly she earned plenty, but it didn't rise to yachts. She thought a gal ought to have a few guys in her life, and poor old Rex had been unlucky!

Gloria moved gracefully around the room, her dress swishing against her legs.

'No, we can't go sailing away, I'm afraid, Dan. I'd love it, but there's my programme. And you have to be in L.A. a lot. We're just poor working people, Dan!'

'It's an idea that'll keep,' he stated. 'Drink that Vat 19. I wanna kiss you!'

She was in his arms some time later. He planted his burning kiss on her red,

red lips. He was an awkward lover. The way he held her was an insult to a man with his experience. He was letting his emotions get the better of him when the cabin door opened an inch.

Dan Sweder did not notice. He was in a blurred world of passion, and figured he was ready to go to town with Gloria. The door opened some more, and then whipped wide open as if explosive had done it.

Too late Dan Sweder jerked out of clinging arms. A gun tried to find space between his ribs. The feeling halted all further movement on Dan's part.

Rick Manton grinned, watching him carefully. Thelma sidled into the cabin, shut the door behind her. Rick said; 'Know us, Dan?'

'You — you — small-time punks! Sure I know you — Rick Manton — but I forget the dame!'

'You shouldn't,' chided Rick. 'That shows you're gettin' too big — in the head! Never forget the dame, Dan. Now Thelma Wain and me figure you're a first-class swine. You deliberately set out to corner the dope racket in town. You put us guys out. You're a bigger menace than the damned cops! Thelma figures you oughta be dead!'

The other started. 'You're crazy! Why, you — '

'We want money right now,' said Rick smoothly. 'We think you ought to pay off for the bad time you've given us.'

'You crazy fool — '

'Quit talking. I reckon you ought to have some dough in this cabin. Let's start looking for it.'

Gloria Grahame backed to the cabin wall and looked like she was about to scream at any moment. Dan Sweder shot her a glance. 'Take it easy, honey. These punks are just sounding off. This guy won't use his gun!'

Rick Manton rubbed the gun barrel against the man's ribs. 'Look, Sweder, you louse, we've been all set to kill you! Get that straight!'

After a tense pause, the other breathed. 'Yeah, I get it. I'll remember, too!'

Rick sneered: 'Don't get ideas that we don't count, Mister Big! We could blast you now or any time. Remember that if you feel like it. Right now we figure we want some of your dough — as a sorta compensation for damage done to our business! All right. You got dough in this cabin?'

'Not a dime!' rapped Sweder.

'The way you say that it sounds like the three bears.'

'Why should I keep dough here — ?' began Dan Sweder.

But Rick Manton had spotted the one picture on the cabin wall. A sixth sense told him why the picture was there. He took two big strides across the cabin, keeping the gun trained on Dan Sweder. With one hand Rick slid the picture along on almost invisible runners and behind it was revealed a wall-safe door.

'Dough is where you find it,' cracked Rick. 'Open up, feller. I guess you got the combination.'

The anger that shadowed Dan Sweder's face told Rick he was on the right track. Rick went over, jabbed the gun into the man's ribs again,

'You want me to use this?'

Gloria Grahame pressed against the wall. With fear in her eyes she watched Dan Sweder move reluctantly to the wall-safe. The man glowered for a full minute. Rick Manton got some more movement into the play by jabbing his gun into Dan Sweder's neck. The man flinched, turned an angry face but reached out for the milled knob on the safe door.

'Get on with it!' grated Rick. 'We ain't got all night. You wouldn't like me to start throwing slugs around in this cabin! Somebody might get hurt. And get it straight — our first idea was to rub you out, Sweder!'

Dan Sweder realised he was listening to grimly real threats, and he started to obey. He turned the combination dial in four separate, deft movements. Rick reached out, after watching intently, and swung the door open.

Dan Sweder had been waiting for that. His hand shot to the interior of the safe. He groped desperately, leaning forward, Rick exploded into action. His gun whipped up, hacked down viciously on

Dan Sweder's head. The man slumped, falling awkwardly against the cabin wall. A stifled scream came from Gloria Grahame. Rick jerked: 'Shut her up, Thelma!'

Then Rick grabbed at the gun which lay inside the safe. Dan Sweder had been after that. But his play had not been good enough.

Ignoring the man lying unconscious at his fect, Rick Manton thrust fast fingers into the safe. He brought out a black box, whipped open the lid. The box was stuffed with Uncle Sam's bills. They were mostly fifty-spot bills, and held by rubber bands. Rick stuffed the money into his pockets. He figured a guy could get a lot of green stuff in a jacket pocket, especially when the bills were fifties.

There was nothing else in the safe that interested Rick Manton. Some ledgers and papers stacked up in a corner. Rick thought what the hell they were no use, and he swung the door shut. Stepping over Dan Sweder, he faced Gloria Grahame. Thelma held her arms. Thelma knew a few roughhouse tricks, but her task was easy because Gloria was weak with shock.

'All right, we're going!' snapped Rick Manton. 'Don't start screeching, baby. We might find you again someday and spoil those looks!'

Most of it was bluff but it had the right effect. Gloria Grahame was speechless with fear. Rick jerked a hand. 'Come on, Thelma! Let's go!'

'What about killing him?' she hissed, pointing at the unconscious Dan Sweder.

Rick stared grimly. A pulse twitched on his temple. He hesitated, almost gnawed his lip. He said sullenly: 'Nope! Not like this!'

Thelma's green eyes glittered. 'You could — '

'Not like this!' he repeated angrily. 'I can't shoot an unconscious guy! Jeeze, Thelma, what do you think I am?'

'You wanted the chance!'

'Yeah! Yeah!' Rick looked sombre and worried. 'Sure, but not this way. Hell, baby, I'm not a butcher — and neither are you. Let's get outa here! We've got some nifty dough.'

Her mood changed and she seemed uncertain. She released Gloria Grahame and moved to the door with Rick. The next moment they were out in the passage, and with the swift change and the colder air they both realised they had to get going. They had to get off the yacht and away from the harbour area.

They reached the deck swiftly enough, but there were two men walking around with the air of men searching for someone. As Rick and Thelma came to the deck and slowed, the two men turned and stared. They both wore peaked yachting caps. Rick knew suddenly they were looking for the man who had done duty at the top of the gangway.

As Rick and Thelma walked to the gangway, one of the men stepped forward.

'Leaving so soon, sir?' The man halted, said suspiciously: 'Hey, you weren't with the gamblin' party! I don't remember seein' you!'

'You're crazy,' said Rick pleasantly. 'I've been gambling all night. I'm unlucky so I'm going.'

'Wait a moment.' The man stretched out an arm. 'You're a phoney. Nobody wanted to leave when I was down there — '

Rick did not intend to wait until the two gorillas had him encircled. Rick impelled Thelma to the gangway. 'Get going honey!' He turned lithely to the other man. His fist swung in a beautifully fast arc. It jarred to an instant halt a second later — on the man's jaw!

The man went back a step. Thelma went down the gangway, flashed a backward glance. Rick shouted: 'Get going! I'll be right behind you!'

Then he turned to meet the second man's rush. Fists thudded into body targets as both men slammed into each other. Rick backed, thought he was due for hell when the other man joined in the fun. He got to the top of the gangway, still backing and keeping fists and splayed hands at bay. Rick dropped his hands to the two posts at the gangway head. He lifted his weight off the ground; swung his legs. His shoes slammed into one man's face with plenty of wham. The man staggered back, rammed his pal.

Rick thought the few seconds were his for a getaway. If he stopped to play around any more, he might not get a second chance. He shot down the gangway. He thought that he had played for time nicely and Thelma would reach the auto just ahead of him.

Rick did not have it all his own way. As he raced along the pier, the two men rushed after him. But Rick was a speedy runner. He could really pound along. The other two men were never gaining on him. There wasn't any gunplay. Nobody wanted it, for it would bring cops. Rick sprinted for the white rail near the entrance to the yacht harbour. He vaulted the rail, dived into his auto. Thelma was there, with an open door and an engine nicely purring. Rick had hardly hit the leather when the Oldsmobile shot away. After that the men behind were just figments of a past. A few seconds had made all that difference.

'Made it, baby! We've got some nice mazuma out of this and no kick from Dan Sweder because he can't go to the cops.'

'He can raise hell,' said Thelma quietly. 'You left him alive, remember?'

'Okay. Let him start raising hell. We've still got a slug with his name on it, and if he comes gunning for us he's asking for it.'

She drove fast along brilliantly illuminated streets. She sliced along Ventura Boulevard; passed the monument to Saint Jose Pasqual and turned up Inglewood. She did not drive too fast. They certainly did not want to attract a motorcycle cop.

'You going to the trailer?' asked Rick.

'Yeah. Home sweet home. We've got to figure some smart moves, big boy.'

'The first one is to move that trailer,' said Rick thoughtfully. 'Dan Sweder will locate us fast. But we could get away now and hide out.'

'Anything you say, Rick. We can move out any time. I'm paid up on that site, luckily.'

All the rest of the way, Rick Manton was thoughtful. Thelma drove into the trailer camp some time later and cut the auto lights. They entered the trailer, switched on the light and drew the curtains. Rick got the money out of his pockets and laid it on a table. He began to make a count.

'Two hundred bills — all fifties. Ten thousand bucks in all, baby! Gee, that's nice lettuce! Get me a valise for this lot, honey. All that dough sure spoils my suit!'

A moment later the money was safe in a small valise. Rick drummed his fingers on the table. 'We're getting out of here. Dan Sweder would track this place down in no time. We're too much like sitting ducks. Let's get the trailer out. We can find a real hideout, and if Dan makes a play we can be ready to hand him that slug with his name on it!'

She agreed. They began to stow all loose articles away inside the trailer. Then Rick went out and backed his auto to the trailer coupling. That done he went around the trailer and disconnected the site electricity and water. Everything went smoothly and twenty minutes later, after notifying the site office, Rick drove out with the trailer in tow.

'Look, we'll get out of town, baby. We can park this trailer up in the Baldwin

Hills and still be near enough to hit back al Dan Sweder. We've gotta get a site where he won't find us. Won't be any lights or water laid on, but what the hell!'

She nodded and sat close to him. She was full of pep and thought all this was damned exciting. They'd gotten some money out of it and maybe they'd eliminate Dan Sweder with a bit of luck. Then the dope racket would be wide open in L.A. The small operator would be able to pick up some loose change.

After twenty minutes of driving they left the built up area of La Brea and began to climb the gradients. For about four miles the road was well-lit, and then it changed to a mountain road and the only light was from their headlights. They were approaching Old Baldy, the mountain set in the Los Angeles area and known to everyone. Strictly speaking the height was named Mount Baldwin.

The gradient and the weight of the trailer was telling on the auto. Rick Manton went on ascending for some miles and then he turned off on to a dirt road. Somewhere they would find a spot to park the trailer.

They did find it; a glade with a spring nearby. This was it.

4

The Deal

It was next morning and Rick Manton and Thelma had spent the night safely in the trailer. All around had been the silence of the deserted hillside. Morning found them fresh and confident. Outside, birds were singing in the nearby bushes; the sky was a deep cloudless void.

Thelma rustled breakfast, and although there was no electricity they used gas from a pressure container. They sat down to ham and eggs, rolls and coffee. They were in love and they were young and they were hungry! Also they had smacked Dan Sweder in the pan and had his dough. They felt good.

'We'll go into town,' declared Rick. 'We'll try contacting some of the old fellers — see if there's a chance of getting some dope to peddle.'

Thelma's green eyes were reflective. 'I

don't see how it can have changed. Dan Sweder's the kingpin of the dope trade in L.A. right now. You know that. You don't really think we'll get anywhere. Not until he's dead.'

'Baby, you're plenty bloodthirsty!' he laughed. 'Still I reckon there's a chance I might contact some guy. Everybody doesn't like Sweder's big-shot notions.'

They were in town an hour later. Rick parked the auto and, with Thelma, walked to a barroom called simply: 'Joe's Beer.' The dive lay on Griffon Street, a quiet alley off Centinella Avenue. Because it was becoming warm and he was thirsty, Rick Manton bought an ale for himself. Thelma Wain had the inevitable martini. They looked around. The barkeep, who had been a source of communications in the past, was studiously silent. He gave them only a glance or two.

'Dan Sweder sure shut that guy up!' muttered Rick, as he sat at a table with Thelma. 'Like a damned clam now. Used to talk plenty once — for a buck or two. Knew some suckers who wanted dope. He still knows the suckers, but Dan

Sweder's stooges get the tips!'

They finished the drinks, sat around a bit and saw there was nothing doing. They went out, got to the auto and tooled into the parking lot of the swank Del Marino some time later. The place was on Venice Boulevard and was the usual white stucco edifice with palms for a background and neons for the night. Inside was redolent of dough, but the main activity of the customers, even in the morning, was drinking. It really wasn't much different from 'Joe's Beer'. Rick thought he might meet some helpful character in the Del Marino.

Half-an-hour later he wasn't so sure. He'd drank a rye and a chaser, and Thelma had sipped more martinis. They'd talked to a slimy little character by the name of Seth Slingoe but Seth had been so evasive about dope contacts he could have doubled for an oiled snake.

And then a man and a woman walked into the Del Marino.

The man sidled in, looked around and then the woman followed, She did not look around until she had sat down at a corner table, and then wished she hadn't. For she was Gloria Grahame, and when she saw Rick and Thelma she gave a violent start.

Rick grinned thinly, looked at the man and wondered where he had seen the phiz before. Rick did not realise he was looking at Rex Rand. He just thought he had seen the face somewhere, but he couldn't place him. And he thought the girl was moving around. First Dan Sweder; now another guy. Still that was the way some dames played it.

Gloria Grahame was scared when she saw the two who had robbed Dan Sweder last night. She was also scared at having to meet Rex Rand, but he had been insistent. She had thought the Del Marino would be a nice secluded place for a talk. She had intended to warn Rex Rand that she could not see him any more. This was to be the final meeting, the brush-off. Having to do this was bad enough without meeting the pair who had robbed Dan the previous night.

Although she used a whisper, she told her actor pal good and firm: 'Look, Rex,

I'm terribly sorry but we won't be seeing each other ever again. It — it — just isn't possible!'

He guessed. 'Another man! Look, Gloria, you can't do this to me. I was counting on our friendship becoming something really swell.'

'You fool! Don't you realise you're in danger even being seen talking to me!'

'There's some damned thing scaring you!' he said angrily. 'I don't believe it's all over between us! Who is this guy? What's his name? I'd know him if ever I saw him again! The damned swine — belting me like that!'

He looked indignant and courageous, ready to face anything for her. There was plenty of ham in it for he was a consummate actor.

Gloria was scared. She glanced at the two who had robbed Dan Sweder and wondered if even Dan's big money was worth helling around in such dirty company. What was she getting into? Should she continue with Dan Sweder? Maybe she was a fool. At least Rex Rand was straight. But he hadn't any money. In fact, he was badly in debt and hoping for his next two pictures to pull him out of the mess.

Gloria was a woman who hardly knew her own mind. She did know she was scared and uneasy.

'Yes, there's a guy scaring you,' insisted Rex Rand. 'The same guy who beat me up. I — '

'Oh, for heaven's sake don't try to be clever!' she hissed. 'You're right — this man would kill you. I — I — don't want to bring you grief, Rex. Just let us forget each other. Believe me it's the best thing to do, Oh, I came here to tell you this Rex!'

'I don't agree! I — I — '

'You're an actor,' she breathed. 'You'd be out of your depth with men like those who beat you up. Why, your face is still bruised! Look, Rex, see those two over there? The man and the girl! That hard young guy and the red-haired girl! They're crooks. Why, they held up Da — a guy last night and robbed him!'

'Your friend!' he flashed. 'The crook! The one who had me beat up. You're friends with a crook, Gloria!'

'I'm trying to warn you!' she hissed, 'I don't want to see you injured, even dead! You're not Superman, Rex. You couldn't play tag with these — these guys. Look again at that young guy over there with the redhead. That's the sort of hard guy you've got to be to play games with the men who beat you up! Now I'm going — and don't ever try to see me again. It's for your own sake, Rex!'

She got up so quickly he could not retain her. In a few seconds she had left the Del Marino. Rex Rand got only to the door. Then, gloomily, he wandered back, cursing under his breath.

He stood at his table and drank off his brandy. He turned, was about to go when he glanced at the lean young man and the redhead.

A moment later Rex Rand walked over to Rick Manton and Thelma. He sat down at their table and introduced himself.

'I'm Rex Rand. You may have seen my films.' He couldn't resist mentioning that! 'I don't know you but I think you might be able To help me.' He smiled. 'Strictly for cash, of course.'

Rick scrutinised the good-looking, fleshy face, noted the cuts and bruises. He suddenly remembered reading about how Rex Rand, the movie actor, had been beaten up by hoods. So this was Rand!

'How'd you mean we might be able to help?' Rick asked.

'Did you notice the lady I was talking to only a few moments ago?'

'Sure,' Rick brought out cigarettes, handed them around, looked at the other guardedly.

'Her name is Miss Gloria Grahame. She's a television artiste — plays the electric organ.'

'Plays around with guys, too!' murmured Rick. 'Okay, what else?'

'She knows you two.' Rex Rand paused. 'At least, to the extent that you tangled with a certain man last night. Now I'd like to know the identity of that man.'

Rick Manton exhaled smoke slowly. 'Why not? What do we care? The guy's name is Dan Sweder, the slob. He's a big shot gangster and runs a dope racket and a gambling yacht. If he's the guy who mussed you up, boy, you're lucky! You could be so easily dead. Anything else you wanna know?'

'Your names?'

Rick grinned. 'Meet the lady first — Thelma Wain. I'm Rick Manton. Anything else, Mr. Rand?'

'Where was Gloria last night?' Rand asked eagerly.

'On a yacht with this guy Dan Sweder. When we lamped them, she was in his arms,' said Rick brutally.

Rex Rand looked furious. 'Yeah? Why, the — the — ' He breathed deeply. 'All right. So she was in his arms! And you were there to rob this guy. Gloria said you'd robbed him. Don't worry about me knowing. I'd like to do this Dan Sweder dirt. Can you describe this guy Sweder?'

'We got our dough,' returned Rick. 'Gloria knew that. And then we beat it. We really want Dan Sweder dead. He's a nuisance. Maybe he wants us dead now. Dan's a lean, medium sized guy.'

'When they beat me up there was a guy who answered to the name 'Zac'.'

'Zac Ortmann — one of Dan Sweder's hoods.'

'So the man who beat me up was Dan Sweder,' said Rex Rand slowly, 'and Gloria is friendly with him. You two have robbed him and are therefore his enemies. You've said you'd like Dan Sweder dead. Well, so would I!'

'A fast and dangerous decision. But maybe it's just talk, Mr. Rand!'

'No. I've got some pride! Physically, I couldn't cope with either of those two hoods — Zac Ortmann or Dan Sweder. But I'd like to see them chopped to bits! This Sweder slob is taking Gloria away from me. Now if he was dead! Look, kill the swine and I'll pay you.'

Rick glanced with a thin smile at Thelma Wain.

'How much, Mr. Rand?'

'I can't get hold of a lot of money at the moment,' said the other hurriedly. 'Say two thousand dollars.'

'Two grand. Double it, and we'll collect when the thing is a fact. It's an extra bonus, anyway, because I got a feeling it's us or Dan — and it won't be Thelma or me!'

'All right, four thousand.' Rex Rand's eyes gleamed and it wasn't an act. 'Make it soon before that swine ruins Miss Grahame.'

'Uh-huh. You got an address, Mr. Rand?'

'Yeah, Padua House, Laurel Canyon, Beverly Hills.'

'Sounds classy. We're moving around, so we ain't got no address. Just for the record where do we find Miss Grahame supposing we ever wanted her?'

'She lives up at Brentwood Park, 323 Sun Avenue.'

'Okay.' Rick expelled smoke. 'The kill's a deal.'

'You'll be careful? Of the police, I mean.'

'Brother, we are always careful — especially of the cops.'

Rex Rand said slowly: 'I'm not connected with you if you fall into the cops' hands.'

'Yeah, you want to kill a guy, haven't the guts and are scared of the consequences,' said Rick softly. 'Like a lotta folks. At some time in their lives, a lotta law-abiding people feel they'd like to kill a certain person. Most of 'em never do because they're scared. But they think that way just the same. Okay.'

Rex Rand tried To look grave but just looked a bit fearful. He rose suddenly, shot out his hand to Thelma and then Rick Manton.

'I — I — leave it to you.'

When he had gone, Rick muttered: 'You bet!'

'What a guy!' exclaimed Thelma. 'But we can pick up four grand. It's a gift, You know that. Dan Sweder will have to go in any case.'

'Sure, sure. Well, we came out to get contacts for the dope racket, but we're mixed with something different.'

'Let's go,' said Thelma. 'We won't pick up any business while Dan Sweder is around.'

They went out of the Del Marino and approached Rick's auto. When about two yards from it, something white moved behind the car.

Rick Manton grabbed the girl's arm and held her back.

'Who the hell's that snooping around the auto?' he breathed. 'Wait, Thelma!'

He shoved lithe fingers under his jacket, gripped the gun in his shoulder rig. He stepped in front of Thelma; approached his auto warily. He could still see the white. There was a man behind the car, wearing a white worsted suit, it seemed. Rick could see nothing else.

Rick walked on with a grim set to his jaw. He didn't believe any guy would start shooting out here in the street, but he couldn't be sure. If this was one of Dan Sweder's hoods, anything could happen anywhere and any time!

Rick took two swift steps around the auto, stopped and stared at a bulky figure. The man, in Panama hat and white suit, flicked back a glance. Rick thought the man was getting to the wrong side of his forties. He thought a punch in the belly would upset the man considerably. But nothing had got to that yet. There was even time yet to be polite to each other.

'Nice morning!' said Rick.

'Yeah.'

'You looking for something?'

'My name is Walt Napier,' said the man carefully, 'and I'm a private detective.'

'That mean anything?'

'Not such a helluva lot,' said the other. 'But let me tell you, Rick Manton, that Dan Sweder is gunning for your guts.'

'Yeah?'

'It's a tip, ain't it?'

'Yeah. You know my name, huh?'

Walt Napier smiled cautiously. 'I know most of the tinhorn crooks in this town.'

'Yeah?' said Rick again. 'What the hell you doing snooping around my auto?'

'I'm working for Dan Sweder.'

'Say that again! Does working for him include tipping me off concerning him?'

'I hate the slob's guts! But I'm taking his dough to keep tag on a dame. That guy kills himself with jealousy over a certain dame.'

Rick thought swiftly. 'Is it the Gloria judy?' he asked.

'Yeah. He should keep her in a cage, he's so jealous. He just hates to think any other guy even speaks to her. How he lives with a mind like that, I don't know — seeing that dame gets around on TV programmes.'

'Very interesting,' said Rick. 'You must have seen her beat it a few moments ago.'

'Yeah. She's been seeing the Rex Rand guy. Sweder will love this!'

'He had Rand beat up once on account of the Gloria skirt. Why not just shut up about this?'

'Sweder is hell,' said Walt Napier. 'I daren't cross him.'

'You take his dough. He's a crook. You might lose that shamus licence one of these days.'

'I'll chance that,' grated the other. 'I've been doing that for twenty tears. I bet that's a long time to a guy like you, Manton!'

'Too far back for me,' drawled Rick. 'Okay. Take Sweder's dough. It mightn't last long. Any more tips about how he's gunning for us? We figured he'd be helling after us, so that ain't news.'

'He's got Zac Ortmann and Jack the Gunner on your tail. I don't know any more than that. I'm a private richard, and I don't work right in with Sweder — just this snoop on his dame.'

'Zac Ortmann and Jack the Gunner!

Jack's just been out the pen a year. Now there's a guy with a chip on his shoulder! Wow! That gink takes a shower with his shoulder rig strapped around him! Thanks for the tip.'

Walt Napier waved a white, pudgy hand and walked away like a man who is watching everything that goes on around him.

Rick turned to Thelma.

'Gee, the characters we meet! Let's get in the auto, honey.'

They got in, sat close together for a moment. He slid an arm around her and grinned at her. Her green eyes gleamed into his dark ones.

Rick Manton switched the mood when he murmured: 'We've got to eliminate Dan Sweder. And we ain't interested in tangling with Zac Ortmann or Jack the Gunner. I don't see any percentage in trading slugs with those two hoods.'

She sat back. 'All right, superman, you got a plan for dealing with Dan the slob?'

'Nope.'

'Sounds great. Well, at least you've got a gun!'

'There's just the original idea of picking him off from that window opposite his office in Pico.'

'Why not try it?'

He nodded. 'Okay. It's still a good notion. He can't suspect we'll be so close. I'll need the long heater for that play.'

'Okay. It's in the car — on the back seat.'

'Sure, sure. Yeah, I guess we could do with the long heater. Sweder has to go. With him outa the way, we could get back into business and start making some green stuff. Sure we've got the ten grand, but with Sweder on the morgue slab we'd pick up another four grand from Rex Rand and open out the dope racket.'

'Okay, what are we waiting for?' she demanded.

He grinned, started the engine. 'Nothing that I can figure out!'

He tooled out of the parking lot a moment later and joined the stream of traffic on the road. The trip from Venice Boulevard to Pico took them along palm-lined streets where sidewalks were busy with shoppers. Yellow cabs and long sleek Greyhound buses filled the roads.

The sun was climbing and the day was becoming warm. Under the Californian sun, L.A. sprawled its eleven miles, a town comprising small townships and suburbs with boundaries reaching up into the Santa Monica mountains and into the desert beyond Pasadena.

But the trip to Pico Boulevard was a comparatively short one. Rick parked the auto on the lot he had chosen as nearest to the office block. When he got out, he was carrying the battered golf-club bag. He had parked the auto so that it was nicely positioned for a quick getaway, if needed.

With Thelma, he walked along to the office block. He looked a big guy, goodlooking, athletic. She was cute enough for wolf whistles, but there were none, not with Rick Manton around!

He reached the block. The door was open. Only the top floors were empty. There were tenants in the lower suites.

They went up the stairs, warily. He carried the battered golf-bag case, taking care not to bump it. They watched for signs of other people who might notice them, but no one passed them on the way down. Finally they were above the inhabited offices. Then they came to the vacant one, the one that gave such a good view of Dan Sweder's office window! They went in, closed the door behind them. Rick put the golf-bag down. He went to the window, taking care not to show himself. He didn't however, expect to be seen. Not by Dan Sweder.

Thelma joined him, and together they stared across the concrete chasm. Traffic crawled and honked below. Across the street were the rows of windows, like blank eyes. Rick pointed one out to the girl.

'That's the window, honey. This is probably a game of patience. I can't see Dan Sweder. Maybe he ain't in his office. Maybe he won't be near the place today. Maybe he's helling around after us. That's a laugh with us right here. Anyway, I'll get the gun set up. If he shows himself at that window. I'll take him!'

'And if anybody comes to this office?'

'You can help there. Stick by the door and watch and listen. If some prospective tenant lamped us with a telescope he'd have a fit!'

5

Thelma is Taken

A lot of time had passed, and Rick and Thelma were bored and grim. The certain sense of strain of watching the blank window opposite wasn't the sort of thing they liked to endure. It didn't suit Rick and it didn't suit Thelma. There wasn't a sound in the passage outside. It seemed no one was looking for an office on Pico right then. And the window across the street was annoyingly blank. Only once was there a movement beside the wide pane, and then, as Rick tensed, the shadow — it was nothing else — moved away.

'I think maybe Dan Sweder ain't in,' muttered Rick. 'If he was, he'd stand at that window and look down. Seemed like his favourite pose.'

'Okay. We wait. There's dough hanging on this, remember!'

'Baby, you sure keep me to the grindstone. Right now I'd like a drink and you — in that order.'

'This isn't a bar-room — '

' — and so?'

'It isn't a bedroom, either!'

At that moment Rick looked out of the window. His grin faded. He hunched and caressed the rifle. He steadied it on the little tripod, began to aim.

Thelma felt a grim excitement pound in her heart. She sidled along to Rick. She didn't speak. She guessed he wouldn't have heard her. He was sighting the long heater, his eyes narrowed on the target across the man-made chasm. She looked straight across at the block opposite.

A man was standing square at the window, looking down. The man was Dan Sweder, sure enough. He seemed to be pondering the fate of the universe, but Thelma thought he was probably figuring out some crooked play.

Rick Manton squeezed the trigger slowly.

Sure as hell he couldn't miss. Sweder was a dead man even if he was breathing.

Almost anybody can press a gun trigger. Gun-happy fools have done it — mostly to their own sorrow subsequently. A trigger mechanism doesn't need brains to operate it. A man just squeezes and then, somewhere, the gun explodes. It's so easy a lot of fools have figured they wouldn't be fools any longer but smart guys if they had a rod. Most of these men have been taken, struggling and screaming, to the electric chair . . .

Rick's gun exploded in a second.

It was the same second in which Dan Sweder chose to move out of his reverie.

Rick Manton didn't know anything about that.

All that Rick got was the noise of explosion, the jerk of the gun, the crash of glass across the road. Then he was hastily shoving the long heater into the golf-club bag. Thelma was at the door. Rick slammed the window shut. He whipped up the battered golf-bag, thrust to the door. With the girl, he went out into the passage; moved swiftly to the head of the steps. They hurried down, conscious of the seconds.

'Right now there'll be hell in that office!' he jerked 'Somebody'll be phoning the cops . . . maybe a cop is there already. Dan Sweder won't be able to do much for himself!'

'You got him?'

'Yeah. Sure, I got him.'

They slowed the headlong flight when they reached the occupied offices on the other floors. There wasn't any commotion; everything, in fact, was normal. Apparently the shot hadn't been heard down here. Rick and Thelma walked out onto the sidewalk. Beyond a small knot of people staring up at the broken window, there was nothing out of the ordinary.

With every passing second they got further away from the scene. There was only thirty yards to the parking lot . . . now twenty . . . and less . . . finally they walked swiftly into the lot.

Rick slid to the wheel, throwing the golf-club bag into the rear seating. Thelma Wain was beside him in a flash. He got the engine purring; rolling out and went as quickly as possible down the street with the other traffic.

They had gotten away.

'Well, now,' murmured Rick, 'ain't all that cute! So we've eliminated Dan Sweder! Just a bit of this and a bit of that and we get results. Let's get back to the trailer. We don't wanna be around. Because if that guy's dead there'll be cops. Cops and cadavers always go together.'

'The way you say that,' said Thelma, 'you'd think it was funny!'

In the Oldsmobile it was a nice easy trip back to the Baldwin Hills. Finally they rolled to a stop in the clearing. They went inside the trailer and flopped down. Rick loosened his necktie.

'Let's eat, baby. I'm starving.'

'In a moment, my man. You may feel like a hungry hubby. But you're not!'

He grabbed her soft arm, pulled her down to him. His lips met hers, and pressed a kiss that was ardour incorporated. Then: 'Baby, I'll help you dish up some food. How's that for a deal?'

For the next few minutes they did not give another thought to Dan Sweder.

Rick thought he had got his victim. That was fine.

They joked and kissed and spread a table with cups and plates and food from cans. Outside there was nothing but greenery and twittering birds. It was easy to forget the grim moment of the exploding gun.

Yeah, the hell-around was so easy if you had a gun and guts and some dough to buy an auto, phone calls, food and clothes. You picked up dough here and there, and when necessary you eliminated a guy — just like that. You didn't look into your conscience too far because even those on the hell-around must sleep at nights.

After the meal they idled. And then Rick Manton got ideas about Thelma. She wasn't unwilling.

More time passed and the day became hotter. Rick changed his shirt and washed energetically in the tiny toilet room. He came out clad only in trousers, looking like some movie hero. He grinned at Thelma.

'Say, let's move again. I get tired being

in one place too long. Let's take the auto down to Beverly Hills and collect our four grand from Rex Rand.'

'Okay. It's quick but maybe it's better not to give him the chance to change his mind.'

'He'd better not try that,' snapped Rick.

Some time later, when they were in the car and the trailer was locked again, he was moody, thinking about Thelma's remarks. Maybe Rex Rand might try to chisel!

In this mood, Rick Manton drove down from the hills again and rolled along to Wiltshire Boulevard, and from there to Laurel Canyon, that suburb of neat but expensive little homes built on big landscape lots.

Padua House turned out to be a stucco affair that mocked a mixture of Spanish architecture and Hollywood ideas. Huge curved windows gleamed in the sun. Rick and Thelma approached a sun patio in which lay table and chairs under a vita-ray glass roof. This was for outdoor living, but right then no one was indulging in this luxury.

Rick walked around to the back of the house. Rex Rand was sprawling in a yellow hammock, a bundle of papers that looked like a script in one hand. He glanced up, smiled uncertainly.

'Hello! Come right in. Sit down, please.'

Because he considered himself a gentleman with the ladies, he got to his feet and made a graceful gesture of invitation to Thelma. 'Please find a seat, my dear!'

Rick gave him it hard. 'We're here to collect, Mr. Rand.'

The other sucked at breath. 'You mean?'

'Sure. I bumped him.'

'*Sweder?*'

'Sure, we had it all set up. That's why it's so quick.'

Rex Rand sat down again, slowly.

'Ah — this — er — takes some getting used to!' he said. 'You must excuse me if I react slowly. I — am not quite so young as you, Mr. Manton.'

Rick thought that was a nice under-statement. Rand was twenty years older than he, if he was a day!

'It's good for you, ain't it?' said Rick brutally. 'With Sweder out of the way the Gloria dame will come to you like natural.'

'Yes, yes,' muttered Rand.

Rick looked impatient. 'Well, we did the job, Mr. Rand. Remember the four grand you promised?'

'Don't speak so clearly,' said the other hurriedly. 'I have servants . . . they might hear. I'll send you a cheque, of course.'

'Can't you make it cash — now?'

'It happens I haven't that amount around.'

Rick looked displeased. 'Well, write the cheque out now. I told you we ain't got an address. Make it out 'to cash' an' we'll collect it from your bank.'

Rex Rand nodded slowly. Inwardly, he was wondering what he had gotten himself into. He knew if he wrote a cheque for four grand it would bounce, and by marking it 'to cash' the damned thing would bounce all the faster. Rex Rand wondered what the young man would do. He was hard. He'd want that four thousand dollars. And when he found it wasn't going to be easy dredging four grand out of a film actor called Rex Rand, he'd become unpleasant.

'Okay, what are we waitin' for?' snapped Rick. 'Let's have that cheque.'

Rex Rand nodded, felt his pockets. He knew he hadn't the book on his person. He'd have to go indoors and look for it. He walked away, and his actor training enabled him to give the impression of confidence.

But Rick frowned after him. 'You were right, Thelma. This guy ain't so happy about paying out.'

When Rex Rand returned, he had made out a cheque. He handed it to Rick with a smile. 'There you are, Mr. Manton — the way you want it.'

Rick examined the slip, noted it was 'to cash'.

'Okay. Let's get going. We can just make it to the bank.' He chuckled. 'You won't want a receipt for this, Mr. Rand!'

The other showed sign of his earlier nervousness.

'I'm not connected with — with this

— this death in any way!' he ended on a vehement note.

'Nope!' Rick stuffed the slip away in his billfold. 'Okay, let's go. Good hunting with the Gloria dame, Mr. Rand!'

As Rick Manton departed, the actor muttered contemptuously: 'Damned low swine! Just a low crook and killer! God, I need a drink!'

Rick and Thelma returned to the Oldsmobile and slid to the seats.

'Let's go get that cash,' said Rick. 'Have we time?'

'Yeah, oughta just make it,'

Less than twenty minutes later Rick presented the cheque at the La Brea branch of the Bank of California. Only three minutes after that an unsmiling manager told Rick in a hushed voice that the account could not meet the amount.

'How about a proportion?' snapped Rick Manton.

'Even the smallest sum is impossible. In confidence, sir, there is a considerable overdraft.'

Rick came out and smiled grimly at Thelma.

'A phoney! Not a dime. Why, that chiseller — '

He stopped. She was regarding him with a taut expression, She held a newspaper, and she thrust it to him.

'I bought this while you were in there. Just read that little account. This is the latest edition.'

His grim eyes found the few paragraphs of print.

MYSTERY SHOT

A rifle shot broke the window of a Pico Boulevard office at midday and wounded Mr. Daniel Sweder, businessman. The police did not trace the marksman, but from the angle of trajectory they conclude the assailant fired from an empty building opposite. Mr. Sweder suffered only a minor shoulder wound.

Rick almost flung the newspaper at Thelma. He got into the auto beside her.

'*Mr. Sweder!* Of all the lousy luck! Gee, I'd swear I got that swine!'

'You did — in the shoulder!'

'He musta moved at the last second!'

'Or maybe you missed!' she mocked.

'Listen, baby, don't rile me! I thought I got him! With that long heater, I shouldn't have missed. The guy must have moved at the last moment.'

'Huh! Then he moved at the right time! It was a near thing for Mister Dan Sweder!'

Rick started the motor. He looked around grimly as if half-expecting violent, unpleasant things to happen. But the street seemed innocent enough.

'Sweder will know who shot at him,' rapped Rick Manton. 'He'll be real mean. First his dough and now a plugged shoulder! Baby, I got a feeling that guy won't like us!'

'Quit talking so much. What're you going to do about Rex Rand's phoney cheque?'

'What can we do? If he reads this — and he will — it's an out for him.'

'Damned chiseller!' she said feelingly.

'Aw let's forget him. We'll have to watch out for Dan Sweder. And another thing: I want to get rid of this long heater.

It's hot now. The cops will have the slug dug outa Dan's office wall by now, an' they'll be looking for the rifle that fired it. So let's make a trip to the pool-room where I can get rid of this long heater.'

Rick made a quick trip downtown to Los Angeles; halted the auto at the curb for a few moments while he took the battered golf-club bag into the third-rate pool-room. He was away about ten minutes. When he reappeared, Thelma Wain was certainly thankful. She hardly knew what was disturbing her. No one had passed who resembled any of Dan Sweder's hoods. It wasn't possible for the racketeer to know they were in this street. Maybe she was getting nervy.

'That's fixed okay,' muttered Rick. 'No questions, no answers — and the cops won't locate that rifle! Let's get going.'

Rick Manton was not quite so confident. He had a feeling that he was having bad luck.

He drove out of the shabby district, got on to a main street. He cruised along, thinking. Thelma glanced at him frequently and, wisely, kept silent.

Suddenly Rick said: 'Okay, we slipped up with Dan. But I can get him again — for good the next time. Now I got some hunches. Sure. Dan will have his hoods out looking for us. So we keep away from the usual dives. We don't want to be seen by some of our old pals. Some of 'em are taking Dan Sweder's dough now. There ain't no percentage in angles with Dan Sweder's hoods. I've said that before. It's the boss himself we want to get. Now there's something on my mind. We haven't seen this house belonging to the Gloria judy — 323 Sun Avenue, Brentwood Park. I'd like to wise it up. She's a lead to Dan Sweder, remember.'

'I haven't said a word,' murmured Thelma

'Okay, okay. So I'd like to know where she beds down. Just to figure it out.'

'She may play around with a few guys,' said Thelma dryly. 'And she may bed down in a lot of places!'

'Cut it out! Now if we could get Dan Sweder to call at this 323 Sun Avenue. Or maybe we might find him there getting solace from his lady-love.'

'You ought to know what a guy wants from his lady-love!'

'I'll remind you of that later.' He stared out of the windscreen. 'Let's go find this avenue in Brentwood.'

Because he was feeling grim he made a fast trip to Brentwood Park. At the foot of the hills he turned off Sepulveda, went along some concrete paved streets until he found Sun Avenue. It was a wide, long road flanked by the usual homes set well back from the paved highway. There was plenty of space between homes up here. The grounds around all the houses were well-shrubbed.

Rick watched the mailboxes and when he saw 323 he drove past and halted some way up the road. He turned in his seat, looked back.

'Nice quiet road,' he observed. 'Let's hope it stays that way. C'mon, baby, get out.'

A minute later they were surveying the house belonging to Gloria Grahame. It was a 'ranch-type', which meant the eight or nine rooms straggled in all directions and sun patios covered every little corner thus formed.

Rick Manton glanced down the street. An auto passed, but it was some harmless traveller. Rick noticed a telephone booth at the corner of the road. An impulsive idea leaped into his mind. It was the sort of thing that appealed to him. He didn't work from blueprints anyway; just hunches, notions and impulses.

'Look, honey, here it is: we locate this Gloria judy, see that she's in her home. Then you phone Dan Sweder, imitating the Gloria dame's voice. Can do?'

'Yes. I've heard her speak, and over the line no one will know the difference.'

'Oke. You'll tell Dan Sweder to get over here right away. Tell him you must see him. You're Gloria Grahame, remember, but don't say too much. But first we got to find out that this skirt is at home. Even if she's at the local Woman's Circle it doesn't matter. But if she's with Dan Sweder the trick won't work. In fact, it'll backfire because he'll have a truck-load of hoods up here in no time.'

'This should work!' she exclaimed, her eyes gleaming.

He grinned. 'Okay, let's start on the

gimmick. I hope the hell it goes all right. Either way, this street won't be quiet much longer!'

Rick Manton walked up the driveway to the ranch-type house. He did not desire to be seen. As quickly as possible he slipped around a corner of the house and halted in the cover of a trellis which was covered with a clinging plant. He wanted to get close to the lounge windows which, he reasoned, were at the back. If he could see Gloria Grahame, that was all he wanted.

A moment later he sidled up to the long window, which indicated a lounge. He stared in carefully.

Gloria Grahame's face stared at him from the other side of the room. He heard the staccato playing of an electric organ. The face changed to a shot of the organ keys.

Rick Manton laughed softly and thought this was screwy. He was looking for Gloria Grahame in person and instead had found her on a television screen. The set was in a corner of the room and a Japanese manservant was sitting cross-legged on the floor in front of it, seemingly interested in this vision of his employer.

Rick drew back. He walked softly around the house and then down the driveway as if he had just been paying a social call. A moment later he was beside Thelma, some yards down the street.

'We can't make that decoy call yet,' he snapped. 'The confounded dame is giving her show over the TV. Good thing I found that out. Makin' that phoney call to Dan Sweder would have brought his hoods up here.'

'What happens then, feller?'

'We wait. In the auto, up the road. That dame will return home after her show, and it won't be long.'

And for the next twenty minutes they sat in the auto and smoked and talked.

After a while the idleness turned Rick Manton's thoughts to Thelma and how they had got together. She was all colour. That soft red hair did things to him. Green eyes fascinated him, and moist red lips were usually his for the taking . . .

One or two cars passed and they had to break it up. And then at last, an auto swept up Sun Avenue and turned quickly into the driveway of 323. In the few moments given to him Rick Manton noticed there was a woman driver and no passenger.

'Okay, she's home. We'll walk down to that call box.'

The afternoon sun was sinking as they walked down the street. Another hour or two and the first of the neons in central L.A. would challenge the remnants of daylight.

'You know what to say,' remarked Rick when they reached the phone booth. 'Just give him the impression you're dying to see him.' Rick paused and laughed harshly. 'That's great! He's the one that's gonna die!'

Thelma entered the booth, got the nickel out of her handbag.

Rick Manton smoked and watched her through the glass.

Unconsciously, he patted the .38 Spanish gun in his rig. That was the way he was thinking.

Thelma came out a minute later. She smiled triumphantly.

'He's promised to come over right away. Asked why I wanted him and I told him I was lonely!'

'Figure he'll swallow that?'

'When a guy thinks he can ease a gal's loneliness, he can't think about other things!'

Rick frowned.

'There's just one thing: he can't drive with an injured shoulder. Maybe he'll take a cab, but maybe he'll get one of his sidekicks to drive him over.'

'Will that be bad for you, Rick?'

'I can slay a hood as well as the boss!' he said grimly.

Together they walked towards Gloria Grahame's house. At she driveway he turned urgently to the girl.

'Look, honey, you go back to the auto. Turn it and wait up the street. You'll know when to drive down fast to pick me up.'

She nodded, kissed him impulsively and then walked quickly away. Rick Manton jerked a quick glance around, saw that no one was noticing him. He stepped up the driveway. Halfway up there was a thick clump of ornamental boxwoods. He slid behind the bushes, found he was neatly in cover and yet could command a good view of the driveway and, indeed, the house.

Rick Manton waited. He did not smoke. He took out the .38 gun and checked it.

He thought six shots emptied into a passing car ought to raise hell.

Maybe this was the end of the line. He wasn't particularly fond of killing, but there was no room in L.A. for small operators in the dope traffic as long as Dan Sweder figured to corner everything.

The waiting gimmick seemed to last a long time. He frowned thought grimly the guy ought to be up by now. Surely the gink wouldn't change his mind! Nope, the time was dragging that was it. Rick looked at his watch. Yeah, there was time yet!

While he waited two autos passed up the quiet road. They were just passers-by. Then he heard the sound of an auto turning up the driveway.

Rick Manton tensed. He peered over

the bushes. The engine whine increased. He heard the zip of tyres on concrete. The next moment the car tore into view.

The vehicle was going too fast. The driver was simply racing up. With this discovery, Rick cursed. He raised the gun and fired at the two men in the front seats. Even as he triggered he knew Dan Sweder was not in the car.

Rick recognized Jack the Gunner as the passenger. Another hood, whom he did not know, was driving. But time and everything was shattered by the exploding gun. Rick saw jagged scars appear on the side-windows of the passing auto. The two men inside seemed to duck. Then the auto tore on and Rick rushed out of his cover.

A tearing sound filled the air as the auto rushed off the driveway and crashed into some bushes. Rick Manton did not wait. Maybe he had killed one of the hoods. He wasn't hanging around to exchange slugs with the other. Dan Sweder had not showed up. There was some fast play here!

Rick Manton raced down to the

sidewalk. He sprinted up the road; wondered why Thelma did not drive down to pick him up.

And then, in a second, he saw the other auto at the top of the street. Two autos — one his own! The one Thelma should have driven down to pick him up. And the other belonged to Dan Sweder, a hunch told him!

Rick swerved to the other side of the street. With his change of direction a shot cracked the air, the slug hissing unpleasantly over his head. He plunged into one of the landscaped gardens and sought cover in the bushes. He ran up the lot, getting away from the road.

He realised Thelma had been captured by either Dan Sweder or some of his hirelings. To race up was to meet a sure death. He couldn't help Thelma that way.

Something had gone wrong. That was an understatement. Instead of Dan Sweder coming out to meet his dame, two carloads of hoods had arrived. So Dan Sweder had guessed the call was a decoy. That seemed impossible.

Something had given him the tip-off,

however. The result was Sweder was safe even if the two clucks in the crashed auto weren't so happy!

Rick ran swiftly down the ornamental garden. He jumped a low, white fence, found himself approaching another house. He was cutting across the development, using the gardens as a shortcut. Maybe he'd find a road. He'd have to get away before someone, scared by the shots, telephoned the cops. Dan Sweder's hoods wouldn't hang around long, either. But they'd take Thelma with them.

He hoped Thelma wasn't dead! He knotted his fists in fury at the thought. Then he had a hunch Dan Sweder would take her away — alive! She'd be useful to the racketeer because he'd think immediately that he could get Rick Manton through the girl.

As Rick thrust down a path screened by a line of beeches, he hoped that was what had happened to Thelma. Because it gave him a chance.

He ran on, saw a narrow roadway beyond a house. He made for it, vaulting a fence, encountering a startled householder in his garden. Rick raced on, reached the paved road and walked fast down the incline. He straightened his necktie, dusted his clothes, kicked some of the soil from his shoes. Some minutes later he guessed he was clear. Dan Sweder's hoods would be away, escaping from the inevitable arrival of the police. The thugs just hadn't time to look for Rick Manton.

Rick walked on, came to a main road, went on until he found a bus stop. He was lucky. A minute later the bus rolled up. It was on a circular trip that would deposit him in central Los Angeles. He got on.

Twenty minutes later he got off the bus at Stausen Street, went into the nearest barroom and downed two ryes. He was grim and taut. He could think of nothing else but Thelma Wain in the hands of his enemy. There was only that one stark fact now. It loomed bigger than a mountain. He wasn't even thinking about how Dan Sweder had known there was a trap for him at Sun Avenue. There probably was an answer to that detail but he wasn't thinking about it.

Dan Sweder had Thelma. Dan Sweder

had Thelma. Dan Sweder had Thelma.

The thought pulsed like that. On and on and on. And right then he hardly knew what to do about it. His brain hadn't started to conjure up plans.

While the numb feeling lasted, he went into an underground toilet and got cleaned up. The rush through the gardens had not improved his appearance. He had to get cleaned up. He did not want a dishevelled appearance to attract attention.

Then when he walked into the street again, he lit a cigarette. He felt better, cooler.

He was going after Dan Sweder. He'd kill the guy. He'd get Thelma free,

It was the last thought which clawed at his heart. Killing Dan Sweder seemed an incidental now. Getting Thelma out of his clutches was something damnably urgent.

Apart from the office on Pico and the yacht, Rick knew Dan Sweder had an apartment in a big block on Culver Boulevard. Where would the guy take Thelma?

He thought a snoop around the yacht

might be a good notion but without an auto it was impossible to get around easily. The public transport was always overloaded and comparatively slow. He'd have to get an auto. It was a good thing he had a billfold of money — mostly Dan Sweder's!

Less than twenty minutes later Rick Manton had hired a Ford sedan from a U-drive depot. After that he hustled. He drove down to the yacht harbour at Santa Monica; got out of the auto and stared at Dan Sweder's yacht with burning eyes. Would Thelma be found on the craft? She might be there, but could he get her off?

Rick walked slowly and warily down the pier. He hadn't gone through the gate; he'd vaulted the white picket fence. As he approached the ship, his thoughts boiled over with the pressure of ideas. Maybe he'd find the girl; maybe not! Could he get on board? Who would he find there? Anyone or absolutely no one?

He thought he and Thelma were really on the merry-go-round. There wouldn't be any excitement in it for Thelma — not now! There might be plain hell!

Seemed it wasn't so easy to kill Dan Sweder. With some kills a guy just triggered, and the ease of it was sometimes unreal. This Sweder slob was having the luck of his kind.

Rick Manton suddenly realised he was close to the yacht. The craft rocked sullenly on the water. He stared down, got the impression there was nobody on board. The craft seemed silent and still.

It was pretty easy to jump down to the diminutive deck. Still no sound or sign of others! Rick moved to the gangway giving access to the cabins below. He thought he would check. If the ship was deserted he would have to look elsewhere for Thelma.

He came down into a corridor and stood listening. With a cold feeling of dismay he got the impression that this was a silent, deserted craft.

He walked along, crepe soles making no sound. This boat didn't sound like the gay yacht of just last night. But it was the same. Only the people had gone.

He looked into the stateroom where the gambling parties were held. The roulette table was covered. The cocktail bar was enclosed on all three sides by walnut shutters.

Rick sidled out. He wondered where the caretaker guy was. Maybe caretaker was the wrong term, but there should be some teller around to watch the yacht.

Rick's thoughts snapped back into a recess of his mind as he suddenly heard clumping footsteps on the deck. He alerted like some wild animal ready to strike. He listened, heard the footsteps clatter on the gangway steps. Then two voices exchanged grunting remarks. They were not intelligible to the listening Rick Manton,

He slid aside a cabin door, darted in, pulled the door after him except for an inch and waited.

He had not expected the men to pass down the corridor, but they did, and it was highly convenient, for Rick was able to get a glimpse of them.

One of the men was Zac Ortmann, looking pretty dressy in a full-cut, drape twopiece suit of light fawn material. The other man was apparently an ape — until Rick saw he had a little more intelligence in his face. But he was a big man in shirt and pants and peaked cap. His hairy arms had misled Rick Manton!

The man looked like he was the custodian of the yacht when the swank patrons of the gaming room were not around. It seemed like he had been away for a moment.

Rick whistled soundlessly and grimly. He thought that tackling these two was like trying to imitate supermen. He'd better beat it while he had a chance. Thelma was not on the yacht, so far as he could ascertain.

Rick Manton slid the door along. He was glad it moved soundlessly. Maybe the wacky users of this yacht needed soundless-moving doors, especially at nights!

He sidled into the corridor, turned to make for the gangway. At that moment he heard Zac Ortmann's laughing, sneering voice from some nearby cabin.

'Dan got the dame but the guy took it on the lam! If he's smart, he won't stick in L.A. because Dan's gonna burn that damned town down to get him. Imagine, he heists Dan's dough an' then tries to plug him with a rifle! And that ain't enough for this punk. He tries to lure the boss up to see his skirt with a phoney message. Only thing that went wrong there was Dan phoned the dame a minute after the call to ask her somethin' an' she knew nothing about it! That was enough for the boss.'

'Got the dame, ya say?' grunted the other. 'What's he figure to do with her? I know a joint in Chinatown where they take in dames an' pay for 'em!'

Rick Manton leaned against a bulkhead and anger blurred his vision. When it cleared his gun was in his hand. He did not remember bringing it out.

'I gotta see this ship is fixed okay for tonight,' came Zac Ortmann's voice. 'Everything's gotta be right for some swank suckers, Dan says.'

Rick Manton eased down the corridor. He reached the gangway and went lithely up to the deck. He glanced around swiftly, did not see more of Dan Sweder's henchmen. He flattened beside the hatchway. He waited.

He realised it would be hellish if he had to mix it with the two men down below. Hairy-arms was probably stronger than an ox. He'd be plenty to tussle with unless he was handed a slug.

But this wasn't night time and it wasn't a quiet alley. A gunshot might attract attention.

Obviously, Zac Ortmann knew where Thelma Wain had been taken. That made Zac a very valuable palooka — too valuable for the safety of his hide!

Rick waited. He knew he was taking some grim risks but there wasn't a blueprint for this sort of work. He needed a big slice of luck, and he usually got it. He wanted luck now because he had those sombre, burning thoughts of Thelma in those hoods' hands.

Rick tensed as footsteps clattered on the gangway steps. Someone was coming up. Rick saw the steelwork vibrate. There was time to beat it. But not for a second did he contemplate that, if the man coming up was Zac Ortmann he was very valuable because he knew where to find Thelma. If it was Hairy-arms, it was too bad.

The man swung up, feet pounding at the steps. He came up fast and ended Rick's conjectures.

The man was Hairy-arms!

It wasn't much use playing tag with him, and it wasn't much use giving him time to recover from surprise.

Rick swung the gun butt at the man's head. He could have shot him dead, but that would have brought the harbour cops and spoiled all chances of wringing information out of Zac Ortmann.

6

Rescue

Hairy-Arms took the blow on his cranium. He looked stupefied for a few moments. Rick rammed a fist-full of gun at his face. By all accounts the man should have sagged a bit. But he didn't. Instead he shook his head like a dog throwing off water and whirled his fists.

The fists were like chunks of rock on the ends of tough rubber. They crashed into Rick's body, fortunately not landing on his face. Rick staggered, clutched at his gun. Then, as the man shuffled up, a gloating look on his face despite the wallops he had absorbed, Rick Manton threw some more blows. He gripped the gun like a knuckle-duster. It was the only way to even up some weight in this contest. Rick's slams hurt the man and drew blood in a red brush-mark right across his face.

Rick thought the hell with this boxing idea. He danced out of the man's way thrust his gun into a pocket. Then Rick bent down and grabbed at a heavy wood bar lying at the edge of the deck. Rick swung it, crashed through fists and battered the man on the head.

The wood bar really staggered the man. Any other man would have been unconscious. Hairy-arms staggered back against the low rail. Rick heaved the bar back savagely; swung again.

This time the crashing bar overbalanced the man. The low rail acted as a fulcrum against his ankles. The next moment the man fell with a splash into the sea.

Rick watched for some tense moments while the man floundered on the surface. The man swam to the yacht. He was acting automatically, dazedly. Rick, who could think, saw his chance.

He raised the bar and brought it down with terrible force. The man sank.

Rick threw the wood baulk from him in disgust. Then even as he turned, he knew Zac Ortmann was clattering up the steps to meet him.

Zac Ortmann was unlucky. When he reached the deck a figure slid close to him, but fast. A gun jabbed mercilessly into his ribs. A hand grabbed one arm.

'Don't move or yell!' hissed Rick, 'I've just disposed of your pal and it could be you next! Now where's Thelma?'

Fear showed in Zac's smooth face.

'How — how — '

'Cut the talk! Where has Sweder taken Thelma? Give or I'll blast you!'

'There's cops around here!' snarled the other.

'Must be dumb!' sneered Rick. 'Because believe it or not, nobody saw your hairy pal go! Your last chance, sucker! Where is Thelma?'

Zac Ortmann was a young hood and as vicious as they make them; but he had a yellow streak like all of them. It flared wide and handsome in the next moment.

'Jeeze . . . don't . . . start shootin'!'

'Okay. Talk and talk straight!'

'Dan took the dame to Pelozzi's place . . . he . . . ah . . . '

'Who the hell's Pelozzi?'

100

'A . . . a . . . gink . . . runs a love-nest on Redondo.'

Rick felt sheer savagery shudder through him. He nearly made an incision in the man's ribs with the gun.

'What the blazes was the idea of that? C'mon, talk!'

'Dan couldn't get her to say where you were hidin' out. He figured she'd talk . . . later. He figured he'd get you through the dame . . . later.'

'Later!' gritted Rick. 'I like the way you say that! Where is this Pelozzi's place? Has it got a number?'

'Yeah. It's . . . a . . . a . . . roomin' house of sorts. 784 Redondo. Aw, for Gawd's sake quit borin' a hole in me! You got what you want.'

'And you're getting yours!' snarled Rick.

He whipped the gun up and rammed it down on the man's head. Unlike Hairy-arms, Zac Ortmann went to sleep immediately. His legs could not support him. He crashed backwards down the companionway. Rick went after him.

Less than five minutes later Rick

Manton had the man securely bound and gagged and locked in a cabin down below. That way, he would not be free to telephone Dan Sweder and warn him of the latest unfortunate happenings.

Rick went along the pier and marvelled that other folks were always so taken up with their own affairs that they failed to notice the most unusual things. So far as he knew nobody had seen the rumpus on the *Green Lady*.

He returned to his hired auto and drove away. The sun was sinking on the horizon. He realised the day was vanishing. But maybe night would bring advantages to a place like 784 Redondo!

As he drove along he thought grimly that an auto was a grand thing. Here he was slicing distance. And distance meant something in the L.A. district. He had just left a rumpus at the yacht harbour and looked like running into a new one on Redondo.

The well-known street ran up the coastline, curving inland at one part. Redondo started well, with well-lighted restaurants, nightclubs and dancehalls.

Then it gave way to hotels and a few stores. Then further on, where the road curved inland the premises became shabbier. The properties were mostly old, and rooming houses seemed to be the favourite ones for the buildings.

Rick Manton halted near 784, examined it grimly from the cover of his auto. A grimy building that could hide almost any vice.

The street was depressing in the half-light. In the west the sun sank quickly. Pretty soon night would drop completely over the city. Night and the city! The time for the greedy, the devilish, the wicked to crawl out of their cracks and seek sustenance. And 784 looked like it could house lots of screwy activities.

Rick Manton shrugged off his sombre thoughts. Unless he could dredge up some cute plan, such thoughts were a waste of time. He eased in the clutch, drove some distance down the street and parked again. He got out the auto, leaving the driving door unlocked. He might need the hired heap in a hurry. And then, again, he might never need it!

He walked back along the street, slowly because he was checking his gun. There was a chance that it didn't click so nicely after using it on Hairy-arms' visage!

Rick thought he was having a bit of luck when, as he reached 784 the door opened and a man stepped out. Rick Manton had never seen him before. The man took no notice of Rick until notice was forced on him. It happened swiftly, impulsively, and was typical Rick Manton.

Rick stepped close to the man before the door shut. Rick swung the gun-butt at bullet speed. It contacted on the man's head. The man must have thought someone had dropped an A-bomb. The man went down like an undermined skyscraper. He lay so still he looked like someone dead.

Rick smiled thinly. The door was still open. All this to get a door open, but it had seemed the best thing to do.

Rick stepped over the body and walked into a dark passage. He was feeling keyed-up, grim, satisfied. True, he had not found Thelma as yet, but he had a hunch he was close to success.

The passage was long, and at least six doors broke one wall. Chinks of light showed around one door. Rick hesitated. He was inside the building, but there were four floors. He couldn't stamp around and arouse all the inmates — not until he had located Thelma.

He listened outside the door with the fringe of light. There was only the ticking of a loud clock; no voices. Nothing here to indicate a prisoner was kept. Rick edged along the passage, found a staircase ran up to the next floor. On the impulse, he went up the dark stairs, A dusty carpet dulled his steps. He reached a landing and got an odour of cooking. Somewhere a radio murmured.

Suddenly a door opened and a woman stepped out. She halted, looked questioningly at Rick. She was wearing only a robe and sandals. He saw her bare legs. He thought they were not too clean. He couldn't be sure. It was just an impression.

'Whadya want?'

'Looking for Pelozzi,' sneered Rick. 'Where is he?'

'Ya ain't been here before?' The scare had gone from her; she just looked curious.

'Nope. I'd know where to find Pelozzi if I'd been here before.'

'Yeah. Well, he lives in the damned cellar, an' lets these rooms.' She slid one hand on her ample hip. 'Ya lookin' for a floosie or for Pelozzi?'

'Just Pelozzi.'

'Lotsa girls in this joint,' she insinuated.

'Yeah? Well, get back to bed, honey. You'll catch cold.'

Rick turned with a grin and began to descend the stairs. She twisted her lips at him, walked away with a voluptuous waggle of her hips.

He went down the stairs again. He thought he'd have to locate Thelma quick. The man he had felled at the door might waken up and yell. To say the least, that would complicate things.

He thought it odd that the owner of the love-nest should live in the cellar, but you never knew with these carrion. The world was full of crazy people. He wondered where he would find the entrance to the cellar. And if he got Pelozzi on the end of a gun would that be effective?

Rick thought it would be.

At the bottom of the stairs he surveyed the row of doors again. One of them would lead to the cellar, he felt sure. There wasn't a cellar entrance in the passage, anyway.

He expelled some breath impatiently. He reached out a hand to the door that showed the fringe of light. He shoved it open and prepared for grief.

But, inside the room, he encountered nothing but the loud ticking clock. The room was lighted by a hanging electric bulb; furnished barely with a table and a few chairs. A dead electric fire filled a dirty fireplace. Rick stepped over matting patterned with dirt; saw at once the cellar trapdoor in the corner of the room. He almost leaped to it.

The trapdoor opened up easily. Rick saw light from below at once and caution slowed him. He worked noiselessly after that. He placed the trapdoor well back and went down the steps quietly, gun in hand.

On the bottom step he halted, his lean, good-looking face tightening into a hate-mask. Thelma was there in the well-furnished cellar, and there was a solitary man, apparently her gaoler. Rick guessed this thin, stooped character was Pelozzi.

Thelma was tied to a chair, not unpleasantly but efficiently all the same. Her red-hair straggled down over a part of her face. Evidently she had been struggling.

She gave a slight start at seeing Rick Manton there on the bottom of the stairs, standing like a vengeful shadow.

The movement warned Pelozzi. He turned. Rick saw his olive face and black eyes and the scared expression. Rick stepped forward, grated: 'Don't shout or move. Don't get tricky or I'll blast you!'

'Rick! Oh, Rick! Get me outa here!'

'Take it easy, baby. You're as good as out.' Rick's tone changed to pure poison. 'You — Pelozzi — get those blasted ropes off my girl! Now — before I fill your guts full of slugs!'

The man hurried to obey. His hands

shook as he stooped over the bound girl. Pelozzi must have been a tall man when young but he curved like a hook now.

'Snap on to it!' rasped Rick.

'I — I need a knife!' The man gulped. 'Don't shoot! I won't give any trouble! I didn't wanna keep this dame here. But you know Sweder — he's the guy who says what goes these days.'

The man shuffled quickly to a drawer in a chest. He brought out a sharp knife. Rick narrowed his eyes and rapped: 'Use it on the ropes, feller. And hustle!'

The man began slicing, fear preventing him from attempting any trickery. The rope fell from the girl. She attempted to get up before all the rope was cut from her, but had to sit back.

It was at that moment when Rick Manton was watching Pelozzi and the girl, that a figure hurtled down the cellar steps in one wild leap.

So swift and furious was the onslaught that Rick was taken unawares. In fact, he was just taken, period. The attacker landed on Rick's back like a truckload of bricks.

Rick Manton flattened to his knees. He gasped for air; twisted to meet the attacker. He got a snap view of Jack the Gunner's big moon face contorted with the emotion of savage hate. Then it was a real scrap. Rick had lost his gun. Jack the Gunner, for some odd reason, wasn't thinking of using his.

As Rick and the hood fought, Thelma Wain struggled free from the remaining rope only to find herself in combat with Pelozzi. Evidently he figured he could handle a dame.

He figured wrong. Thelma was a fury that clawed and kicked and slapped. Pelozzi soon found grief. But he kept her occupied and she was unable to help Rick Manton in any way.

Rick had gotten over the disadvantage of being taken by surprise. But Jack the Gunner was a tough proposition. It seemed he could use his fists as well as guns. And the way he used them proved he knew every lowdown trick in the roughhouse game. The two men rolled over the cellar floor and sent a table crashing to one side. There was a fire

110

— an electric one — burning at the centre of one wall. As they rolled, Jack the Gunner attempted to force Rick's head against the red-hot elements. Rick was on his back, the other at his throat. The fire was only inches away.

Rick rolled his eyeballs desperately; felt the heat evaporate the sweat from his brow. He thrust at the other man's deadweight; kicked like a trapped animal. Jack the Gunner lost balance; they rolled again, this time Rick on top.

Because it was Jack the Gunner's idea, Rick figured what was sauce for the goose was sauce for the gander. So he thrust viciously, humping the man nearer to the red-hot twin elements. Jack the Gunner burst a fist into Rick's face. Blinding lights slashed furiously through Rick's head. But he kept his relentless grip on the other man. Jack the Gunner, at a disadvantage because of Rick's weight upon him, used his free arm again. Another blow sent bloody lights blinding Rick's eyes and brain. Rick just took it. He held on grimly, spat and waited until his vision cleared. It did and while Jack the Gunner was using his arm as a lever to get a chance to escape, Rick thrust with tensioned legs. The movement brought Jack the Gunner closer to the electric fire. It was like shoving a weighty burden along. Rick heaved again . . . another inch . . . and then an animalistic howl of agony tore from Jack the Gunner's throat. A terrible smell of scorched skin rose slowly. Rick gritted . . . thrust again . . . almost blindly.

Thelma Wain heard the screams and wondered what was happening to cause the inhuman sounds. Pelozzi was doing his best to keep her busy. Thelma knew it wasn't Rick who was screaming. That was good enough.

She got sick of Pelozzi. He was a hateful slob. Anyway, a two-legged rat. She retaliated with special strength, clawing at the man's eyes. He didn't like it. And when Thelma kicked him where it hurt most, he buckled up like a moth-ridden concertina. He staggered to a wall and folded like a man made of rotten sticks. Perhaps he was rotten at that.

Thelma jumped triumphantly to Rick

Manton's aid. She picked up the first thing to hand — a heavy boot lying beside a chair. She leaned over the two struggling men and swung the boot. The heavy sole struck against Jack the Gunner's head. He gasped horribly, and his eyes rolled and dilated as he stared up in stark fear at this new attack. Then Thelma swung again . . . and again . . .

Rick rose, jerked a glance at Pelozzi gibbering in a corner. The man looked like he was trying to get through the wall. Rick swung his gaze back to Jack the Gunner. What he saw sickened him, so he looked at Thelma instead. Jack the Gunner was alive, but maybe the gink was wishing he wasn't!

'Let's get outa here!' snapped Rick.

'Oh, Rick, are you all right?'

'Sure, sure! But you, baby — are you okay? Have these swine hurt you? If they have — '

'No, I'm okay, just scared.'

'You don't look much scared — not you, baby. The way you damaged this guy. Quick, let's go — '

They thrust towards the stairs. They

went up quickly. In the lighted room, Rick paused to tip down the cellar trapdoor. He thought the two down below would not raise the alarm for some time. Pelozzi looked mighty sick. Jack the Gunner was a fearful mess. Maybe it would be better if Jack the Gunner was left dead, but there was not time for that now, even if there was inclination. It seemed the man had been sent by Dan Sweder to see if Thelma was sufficiently scared to talk. Or maybe some other reason. Whatever it was, the gink would be wishing some other man had got the job.

The cellar had been a soundproof battleground for there was no indication that any of the other inhabitants of the cathouse had heard a thing. Rick and Thelma went straight to the front door. Rick remembered the man he had struck. He wasn't to be seen. Seemed like he had picked himself up and beat it. Strange the reactions of various folks. Some would have raised hell; this one had taken it on the lam.

Another few moments and Rick and

Thelma were hurrying up the street to Rick's hired auto.

They flopped into the front seating and gasped with relief. They were both mussed up pretty thoroughly. Thelma's clothes were torn; she looked like a bedraggled heroine from a B-grade movie. The upper proportions of her voluptuous figure were barely covered; Pelozzi had fought like a woman tearing and scratching instead of dealing blows. Rick Manton wasn't a pretty sight. No man can rough it with another husky fellow and get away without plenty of bruises and torn clothing. A lapel of Rick's coat was ripped right down. He figured the coat would suit a scarecrow now.

Rick fumbled for the dash controls. He thought it was a good thing he had left the key in the dash; otherwise he might easily have lost it during the scrimmage.

He started the engine; tooled away quickly. He realised they were not really away until there were great chunks of distance between them and the cathouse on Redondo.

They both had plenty to say but the first things said were very personal.

'Gee, sugar, I'm glad you're outa that dump!'

'Rick — oh, Rick, I'm so happy! You got me out! I knew you'd get me free!'

'I couldn't rest, baby. I got a lead on to you when I was down at Dan Sweder's yacht.'

'Sweder figured to get you through me, Rick. He wanted to know where we had a hideout. He'd discovered I owned a trailer. He didn't know where it was. I wouldn't talk.'

'Did they try to hurt you?' Rick jerked a savage, inquiring glance at her.

'A bit. Sweder thought he'd get you through me some time later.'

'That slob ain't never around when there's any rough play, I notice,' grated Rick Manton. 'I grant you he got the better of us with that phone call from Gloria Grahame's place. I should have known he'd phone the dame again!'

'Forget it, Rick. Let's get back to the trailer and relax. I feel tired, mussed. I feel sick of the hell-around.'

'I got that feeling, too,' admitted Rick.

They were human, and almost too much had happened that day. Given half a chance, most folk pack in somewhere along the line even if only to return to the fray when refreshed. Rick and Thelma felt they'd had enough. They still figured to get Dan Sweder — but some other time, thank you.

'What the devil did Sweder do with my auto?' asked Rick suddenly.

'It was driven away. Probably he stuck it in some garage.'

'Most likely give it to one of his hoods to sell to the stolen auto receivers!' growled Rick.

He drove through the lighted streets, where neons flashed green and red light into the sky. They passed a million winking advertising signs. Car lights passed from the opposite direction to a continuous stream. People were driving out for their pleasures most of it innocent enough and akin to the habits of others in big cities.

After twenty minutes fast driving on the big new freeways those wide, sweeping concrete roads that soar like railroad bridges across congested areas — Rick Manton took the car up into the Baldwin Hills. The city lights dropped behind and remained only as a carpet of stars when looked at from the heights.

Soon they reached the trailer. They went inside, flopped down.

'Hell, I'd like a drink, baby!'

'Me, too. Aw, damn Dan Sweder! Damn everything about him — '

Some time later they were silent. They had cleaned up and changed clothes. Rick put on a Californian sports coat of many hues and blue worsted trousers. Thelma looked attractive in an inexpensive cotton dress. They were hungry. They started to make a meal, with coffee, canned meat and canned fruits.

'For the rest of the night we sleep,' said Rick. He grinned. 'Well, most of the night!'

7

The Trap

The sun-up brought their problems back to mind again. They dressed, kissed, ate and were reflective. Rick summed it up.

'We've gotta get back into the mill, sugar. We can't just sit up here in the wilds. We're fighting a guy and attack is the best defence.'

'Okay.' She smiled assent. 'What happens?'

'We go downtown. We buy two guns — one for each of us. I lost my gat last night.'

They left the trailer some time later and motored down from the hills into the built-up areas. He drove into Alameda Street, to a little gunsmith store where he knew the proprietor would be accommodating.

Fifteen minutes later he was supplied with two .38 Smith & Wesson automatics and two boxes of slugs and no officious questions. He didn't sign anything. He just walked out, grinning, and came to Thelma.

'Here's a heater for you, baby. You know how to use it. Remember, it's for Dan Sweder or his louses. We're not gunning for innocent cops or other folks who have nothing to do with this hate-feast.'

They smoked, sitting inside the car. Rick said suddenly: 'It's Sweder we want. We just want him eliminated so we can get back to making some dough. And it ain't just that now. He'll have a neat little hate for us. He's got the mazuma to hire hoods and gunnies, and he'll do just that. So we got to get him first.'

Thelma Wain said: 'Gee, I wish we had an organisation and could hire gunnies!'

'We don't want some lunkhead that we can't trust!'

'You got any ideas, Rick?'

'Yeah.' He grinned. 'Always got ideas, I guess, even if they don't always work out okay! How's this: we snatch the Gloria Grahame dame and make Dan Sweder

120

hop like he made me hop when he got hold of you!'

Thelma Wain showed white teeth in an uncertain smile.

'You think that will get Dan Sweder? Remember it's that guy we want to do dirt. We don't particularly want to hurt anyone else.'

'You think the idea no good?'

'Put it over if you want to, Rick.'

'We came unstuck the last time we went near that dame's house,' he grunted.

'All right — think up another idea!'

'Dan Sweder has an apartment. Now maybe we could find the louse there?'

'No use,' she said decisively. 'Too many neighbours. People see you come and people see you go.'

'Okay. How about letting the palooka see us? How about a phonecall just for the purpose?'

'You mean — ?'

'We'll give him the raspberry over the line and tell him to come out and get us.'

Thelma smiled eagerly. 'Now that sounds like real Rick Manton! Well, it'll cost only a nickel to try it! What are we waiting for?'

'Nothing. Just a call box.'

Some five minutes later Rick was dialling Dan Sweder's office on Pico Boulevard. He got through to a male voice immediately. It was Dan Sweder. The man did not hire any woman, not even a secretary.

'Hiyah, Dan,' sneered Rick. 'Know who it is? You hate my guts. I'll give you one guess.'

'Rick Manton!' breathed the voice. 'Look, punk, you think you're smart but I'll break you and have you sliced in a concrete-mixer! You — you — '

'Remember, Dan, this is a public phone,' mocked Rick.

'Say, you rat, you robbed me, I've lost two guys off my yacht because of you!'

'You'll find the guys in the bay,' sneered Rick. 'The Pacific always sends 'em back!'

'Zac Ortmann wants your guts! And Jack the Gunner is gonna get you, punk You're a dead guy!'

'I feel mighty fine!'

'What's the idea ringing me like this,

anyway?' snarled Dan.

'Just wanted to say I think you stink, louse! I don't think you're a big-shot. You're punk, Dan! You just got big ideas, that's all, and a lotta luck. You won't boss the snow business in L.A, much longer.'

'The way you talk — ' Dan Sweder came back with a poisonous sneer.

'Yeah, yeah. Well, Dan, I need a drink. I'll drink your health in the *Ringing Bell* on Vermont. So long, snake!'

Rick cradled the instrument and laughed good-humouredly.

He thought the call had been a joke. He had enjoyed stringing the man along. If he fell for the spiel, he was a sucker. But it looked like Dan Sweder had taken the whole thing in earnest. He had sounded like a rattler with an ulcer!

Rick Manton looked up across the road at the beer-joint called the *Ringing Bell*.

Maybe the inn would ring before long, but it wouldn't be joy bells. It could be, however, a death knell!

Because Dan Sweder wouldn't let it pass. The man had some guts. To boss a dope racket a man had to have belly muscles. And Dan would be out right here, to see what was cooking at the *Ringing Bell*.

Rick left the phone booth. A fat woman went m after him. She handed Rick an indignant look because he had kept her waiting. He wondered how she'd react if he told her he was fixing to kill Dan Sweder.

Rick went out to see Thelma. She was sitting in the hired auto. She smiled at him as he came up.

'Well, big feller? How did it go? I was watching you and I think you got in touch with him.'

'You bet I did!' And Rick Manton told her all that had been said.

'That will give him the bellyache,' said Thelma. 'We'd better figure out something in case he comes over with his gunnies fast.'

'We don't figure out anything. We take the auto down a side street and wait for Dan's sedan to roll past. We know which way he should come.' Rick pointed. 'Soon as we see him driving past we go after them. You can drive and I'll shoot. Maybe

I'll have better luck and get him this time.'

'Okay, Rick.'

'It's the best thing for a quick getaway,' he explained. 'We're moving all the time. Soon as I give him the slugs we can be tearing away. There won't be any reaction quick enough to stop us.'

Rick Manton drove the car to the side street that he considered would be a sure vantage point. An auto coming from the direction of Pico Boulevard would surely pass the side street.

They parked the car after he turned it so that the auto pointed up the street. They sat grimly silent and smoked.

After a minute he threw his cigarette away and started the engine again. Then he got out of the car and Thelma sat behind the steering wheel. Rick Manton got into the other seat. He eased out his new gun, gave a few moments of inspection to it.

'Move the auto up a bit, sugar,' he advised. 'I got a feeling Dan Sweder ought to pass up Vermont any minute. Soon as you sight his auto, snick into gear, and drive fast after him. Leave the rest to me.'

'Gee, I hope we have plenty of luck!'

'You bet. You scared? Don't get that way, baby. You know this racket is chancy. With a bit of luck we'll lick this guy. He asked for it an' I figure he'll get it.'

'I don't like the waiting, Rick.'

'You won't have long to wait, I guess,' he answered grimly.

She crouched at the wheel. They were both watching every passing vehicle. She was ready to send the auto forward instantly. Once she thought a passing auto contained the man they wanted; but it was a false alarm. She braked. The car had moved only a foot. They waited again, grim, watchful, and ready.

And then, almost magically, they saw the sedan moving at a fair speed over the intersection and at the same time Thelma Wain let the hired auto spring forward. Within a second their car was close to the sedan, Thelma swung the car out to pass close so that Rick could start some deadly shooting

They had seen four men in the sedan

and one of the men was undoubtedly Dan Sweder. He was not driving. He had Zac Ortmann by his side doing that chore. Of course, Dan Sweder had a wounded shoulder. That had not stopped him coming after his enemies. Rick had not thought the plugged shoulder would stop him.

Thelma Wain fed gas to the auto engine. The car gained on the other vehicle. Rick poised, crouching at the lowered side window, gun in hand.

The other sedan was slicing up to the *Ringing Bell* tavern. The driver evidently figured to stop abruptly. Thelma fed more gas. She was not quite abreast of the sedan. But in another couple of seconds she would have the hired auto level with Dan Sweder's sedan. Then Rick would empty his gun at the man they wanted.

At that very moment, to Thelma's instant consternation, a woman darted from a traffic island. In a second she was directly in the path of the hired auto. It was incredible that anyone should jump into a roadway without hardly giving a glance but this woman had done that.

What made it worse, she was carrying a baby in her arms. She looked an impoverished woman; maybe one of the many migrants who came to the Golden State looking for the land of plenty.

All this Thelma observed in a split second; like the flash of a camera shutter. She heard Rick's frantic shout:

'Watch out! That woman! Thelma, don't hit her!'

Then Thelma wrenched at the steering wheel, all thoughts of Dan Sweder's sedan completely pushed from her mind.

The hired auto sprang like an animal. Even the chassis seemed to twist. To Thelma there was a confused vision of the woman with the baby and then that changed as the auto crashed into the traffic island standard. The windscreen instantly changed into a pattern of starred glass. There was noise and grating metal; then Thelma was thrown against Rick Manton.

The crash was not so serious as it might have been because Thelma had braked violently. But the auto buckled into the standard. Thelma felt her legs knock painfully against the steering column. She snapped her eyes shut; heard glass tinkle somewhere. Then, in seconds, it was all over. Rick Manton, unhurt, thrust a door open, turned and helped Thelma get out of the car. She slid out, felt his arm supporting her. She heard him mutter: 'Let's get away from here, baby, but fast! Think you can make it?'

'I'm all right, Rick!' She heard her own voice faintly.

She knew Rick Manton would not want to stop to answer questions from cops.

They were lucky to get away. People were coming in all directions with the intention to help or merely gape. Rick, one arm around the girl, pushed past them. Luckily they allowed him to go. There wasn't a cop as yet to detain them.

In seconds Rick and Thelma had reached the sidewalk. They went down an alley swiftly, turned another corner, anything to get away quickly.

'Hell, baby, that was bad luck!' snapped Rick. 'But you had nothing else to do. You couldn't have hit that woman!'

'I — I — hardly know yet what

happened!' stammered Thelma. 'I just twisted the wheel, I guessed we missed the woman and the baby!'

'Yeah, we missed her!' Rick cursed. 'Damned stupid thing to do, just step off like that! Hell, we were all set to obliterate Dan Sweder, too. Another moment and we'd have been level with his sedan. I'd have got the slob for sure.'

'Looks like Dan Sweder kept his auto moving.'

'Yeah. One thing I know — that bohunk wouldn't have crashed a car to save a woman and a kid.'

Rick and Thelma walked on swiftly, taking a number of small streets. They were now well away from the scene of the crash. It seemed they were getting away from any possible awkward questions.

'Guess I'll lose the deposit on that hired auto!' grunted Rick. 'Won't be any questions that end because I handed out false name and address.'

'You got your gun?' asked Thelma.,

'Sure.' He grinned at her, 'I always hang on to my gat — well, most times. And you?'

'It seems crazy,' she said, 'but I got out of that crash still clutching my handbag! My gun's in the handbag. How'd you explain a crazy thing like that?'

'An unconscious reflex,' he said. 'Dames are always reaching for handbags. It's part of their lives. It's crazy, sure. You tell somebody about this and they probably won't believe you!'

Within a few minutes they were back on a main road again. There was a streetcar service, one of the few remaining lines in L.A. They jumped on simply to get away from the area.

They got off the streetcar and went into a restaurant for coffee and a chance to think things out. They sat down, Rick thrust fingers through his thick black hair.

'Here we are, two people on this lousy run-around! Well, we ain't got Dan Sweder yet. The luck of that guy!'

'We need another auto,' Thelma pointed out. 'I didn't like riding that streetcar. It's so damned slow.'

'Guess I'll hire another. Maybe I'll get my own car back some day. Maybe. Good thing we got that dough off Dan Sweder.

Say, he'll discover we were in that crash — you can count on that.'

Thelma's green eyes smiled. 'Maybe he'll be hoping we're hurt. He'll find out we didn't break our necks. Well, what now, Rick? You still want to kill Dan Sweder?'

Rick drummed fingers on the table; looked up at a waitress who brought the coffee and rolls. Then, later: 'Sure. Look, honey, maybe we could operate in some other town, but it would be like starting all over again. Now right here in L.A. we have old contacts and pals. If Dan Sweder were eliminated his organisation would fall to bits and we small people could work like we used to do. Say, do we just fade out because a gink like Dan Sweder gets big ideas? Do we fold up because that feller figures he wants all the trade? So people want dope. Sure, they're crazy. They got no right to want dope. But they do. And if they don't get it off us they get it from other people. Dan Sweder is just plumb greedy. He wants all the profits.'

'And what's your conclusions, my hunk of beefcake?'

'We go after Dan Sweder. We get him, somehow, sometime. We gotta think up a new gimmick, though — he'll be leery by now!'

'Yep. But we can get him. And for good.'

'Uh-huh? How? You got any notions?'

'Yes. A neat one. How about snatching this Gloria dame, like we thought of before?'

Rick stared reflectively at the table-cloth.

'M'mm. So we snatch the dame, get Dan to come out and rescue her. Then we blast the slob. Well, I don't know that it'd work.'

'Why not?'

'Well, honey, he can hire so many thugs we just couldn't cope if he brought them all along on the rescue stunt.'

'Are you protecting this Gloria dame?' she demanded.

'Baby, I don't care anything about that dame. She's playing with fire, anyway, fooling around with a guy like Dan Sweder.'

'All right, figure out something else to

get Dan Sweder! But I sure hope it's something that works because I'm getting tired of this run-around.'

'Look, honey, let's get outa here,' said Rick. 'Let's go hire another auto, and go see if we can get a supply of dope from Madgy Helpin. She always played okay with us in the past. She might get us a few ounces and we might be able to sell 'em. At least we have some customers — and if they need the stuff at least customers don't take orders from Dan Sweder.'

Thelma Wain nodded. 'All right. Madgy Helpin might be a pal, but I know that she is getting supplies from Dan Sweder. Still, we used to he good friends. Okay, let's go see her.'

They left the restaurant and walked a few blocks. The sidewalks were crowded with people; the bright Californian sun was playing on the white buildings. From empty patches of ground tall palms sprouted. Rick Manton took Thelma along until they located an auto-hire garage. As they stopped and stared, a man in a mustard suit came out to give them the business. Rick said sure he wanted to hire a car. That was enough for the pressure merchant.

'You can get one here. Fastest service in town. Where else can you hire an auto in five minutes?'

That was okay with Rick Manton. Some more of Dan Sweder's dough went in a deposit on the auto. Rick signed 'Terry Delano' on a slip. He remembered the name from a screwy radio pro-gramme. There wasn't any fuss. The auto — a three-year-old sedan — was filled with gas, and Rick drove Thelma out some time later.

'Maybe I should have bought the heap,' he muttered. 'But I still got hankerings to get my Oldsmobile back.'

He drove across town, cutting down Slausen Avenue, turning along Western. Here were straight streets intersected by small lanes and alleys. There was a lot of old property, and the surveyors in the Civic Centre had no record of half the strange old properties.

Madgy Helpin lived in one of these old places. The rabbit warren she owned just

135

wasn't on any record. The cops would
have loved it if it had been!

For Madgy Helpin ran a sort of
doss-house for crooks on the run. Any
palooka who wanted to hide out for some
time usually ended up at Madgy Helpin's
dive. She had her dirty hands in a lot of
sidelines, too. Dope, vice, murder, mug-
gings, were all sources of little profits to
Madgy. She never made a big cut from
any deal. But she had been making steady
profits for years. No one knew what she
did with the dough; although it was
rumoured she had a son who attended a
swank academy in the Midwest.

Rick and Thelma were talking to the
tall, angular female some time later, the
hired auto discreetly parked in a nearby
alley.

'Say, Madgy, you got any snow you
could sell us? We gotta few customers we
want to supply.'

The woman's sour brown eyes looked
back reflectively at them.

'You know it's hard to get dope now
unless you got an in with a certain guy.'

'We know that, Madgy,' returned Rick.

'That's why we're here. We'd sure appreciate it if you could sell us some supplies.'

There was silence, Madgy Helpin smoked a yellow cigarette and blew out smoke into the close atmosphere of her room. It was a cellar room. It was oddly shaped and there were three doors leading off. Rick knew they went to passages, and from there access to some disused sewers was possible. In fact, he was willing to bet there were guys hiding out in the sewers right now, in elaborate cellar-rooms that had never seen the light of day.

'Okay,' muttered the woman, and her lean, mannish face scowled. 'I'll sell you some snow. I sure hope a certain guy don't hear about it. He wouldn't like it. You know the feller I mean?'

'Sure,' said Rick viciously, irritated by the thought that Dan Sweder's power was felt right through to this woman. 'Sure we know the guy. A slob called Dan Sweder! Who the hell does he think he is! I tell you, he won't ramrod the dope racket for much longer in L.A.!'

'He's just about the boss at the moment,' muttered Madgy Helpin. She looked up, a sour gleam in her eyes, 'You kinda got a hate for him, ain't you, Rick Manton?'

'I wish to hell he was dead!'

'Heh-heh! Well now, I wouldn't be worried about this feller if he hit a morgue slab, either!'

'He poisoned some business for you, Madgy?'

'I don't like him!' snapped the woman. 'He's too big! Sure, he's been spoiling things for me, too!'

'What sorta things?'

'Never mind. You do him some dirt and I'd like it but — ' She looked cunning — 'I ain't connected with you!'

'All right Madgy, just get us the dope,' said Rick sardonically. 'And leave Dan Sweder to us.'

The woman rose and went to a black chest of drawers. She was wearing a black suit. The skirt and jacket looked like she slept in them. She was tall, thin. Her hair was thin and wispy. If she had a son, he'd have difficulty calling her 'Mammy'.

She returned and carefully placed some clean, white paper packages in front of Rick Manton.

'You can have this lot for two hundred bucks. You oughta make a neat profit outa this lot.'

'Yeah. Like hell. You're the one who has made the profit, Madgy! Okay, we'll take it so we can open up some trade.'

Rick peeled off the bills and paid the woman. She noticed the roll in Rick's billfold.

'Thought you were having a bad time, Rick Manton?'

'Sure, sure. But we still got some mazuma.' Rick put the packages in his pocket. 'You know, Madgy, you got a queer joint down here. I hear you got some real amazing places under these floors.'

'What's it to you? You and your gal don't wanna use my cellars!'

'You never can tell. Okay, we'll get going.'

Rick and Thelma left the place and were shown to the door by Madgy Helpin, not out of politeness but because she liked to look occasionally at daylight.

Rick and Thelma wandered back to their hired auto and climbed in. Rick started the engine.

'We'll phone some people and trade this stuff right away. The profit would be okay if it was steady. But it won't be steady as long as Dan Sweder has everything cornered.'

For the next hour they made some careful calls on certain people whose names were often in the Who's Who directory. Following the phone call, Rick and his girl called on the person, and left a few ounces of 'snow'. There wasn't a great deal of trouble in disposing of the small amount of dope. Of course, Rick and Thelma had spent a lot of hard graft in the past in raking up these contacts.

Rick Manton and Thelma Wain never considered that the dope was doing terrible harm to the people who bought it. They thought the folks were suckers to take the stuff. In most cases, they were people with more money than sense whose crazy habits had gotten them into the dope game. Rick considered he wasn't to blame for the vicious habits of society wastrels.

At the end of the hour's work they had only an ounce of the stuff remaining in their possession. They had sold the rest for cash. Considering the time put into it the thing was easy money.

They leaned back in the auto. Rick lighted a cigarette, Thelma lit one, too, but after inhaling for a moment she stubbed it in the dash tray.

'I get sick of smoking! There oughta be something different. Say, I wonder what that snow is like, anyway. Let me have that packet, Rick.'

She held out her hand, smiled into his eyes.

Then she saw them change into glittering, angry marbles.

'You ain't gonna get any damned packet anytime, no time! You think I'd let you take that blasted stuff, you're crazy!'

'But — '

'Don't ever be such a fool, Thelma!' he hissed. 'I'd sooner beat you within an inch of your life than see you take dope!'

'We sell it, don't we?' she retorted.

'That's different. I'm telling you — don't ever talk to me about tasting that dope.'

She fell into silence. She brought out another cigarette from the pack in the dash compartment and lit it.

Rick stared moodily out of the window.

'We ain't gettin' any nearer to eliminating that Sweder slob!'

8

Renewed Attack

Thelma Wain had a reply to Rick's remark.

'I still think you could get him through that Gloria dame. That guy is insanely jealous of her, ain't he?'

'That's the set-up.'

'Okay. What else do we want? Listen: if Dan Sweder thought some good-looking guy was up there at 323 Sun Avenue making love to Gloria Grahame, he'd be snooping around mighty fast.'

'Go on, baby, this sounds like it is going to be good! Who is going to be the good-looking guy? Not me, because that dame would never swallow that.'

'This dame would never allow it either,' snapped Thelma. 'No, I figure the good-looking jerk should be Mr. Rex Rand.'

'The chiseller. The guy who hands out phoney cheques.'

'Never mind that now. Now if Dan Sweder thought that elderly ham was fooling around with his judy, he'd be up to Sun Avenue as fast as four independent-sprung wheels could take him.'

'Yeah?'

'Sure. That's the set-up. Naturally, we'd be hanging around Sun Avenue.'

'Just like the last time?'

'Just like the last time, m'boy. But we'd be together. I don't want to find myself back in Pelozzi's cellar!'

Rick nodded coolly.

'All right, let's try it. We go to see Mr. Rex Rand. I don't think he'll be happy to see us.'

Rick Manton was secretly glad of some kind of activity He was grimly annoyed that Dan Sweder had not by now joined his pals in Hades. Following Thelma's suggestions, he had some sudden ideas about such a decoy set up.

He drove out of the quiet road, joined the endless stream of traffic through central Los Angeles.

Twenty minutes later the bright afternoon found them in Beverly Hills. Rick drove along Laurel Canyon and wondered how people afforded such swank living. He got a sudden notion that he and Thelma had no class; they were brittle people without any background. They were products of big cities; they didn't even have a regular job. They were outside the law. Rick gave a curt little laugh that puzzled Thelma because she could not read his thoughts. He thought what the hell, he'd be wanting to settle down next in a stucco bungalow and marry the gal and raise kids!

Rick halted his hired auto a little way from Padua House. He thought it a good idea that Rex Rand should not be warned of their visit. It was always a good point to take a guy by surprise.

It happened the actor was at home, reclining in a hammock on the sun-patio. Rick thought the man did a lot of resting. Well, that was one way to avoid ulcers. Rex Rand got to his feet in a hurry, however, when he saw Rick and the girl.

'Good afternoon! Er — what brings you up here?'

'You, Mr. Rand.'

'Me?' The actor seemed nervous. Then apparently he remembered he owed Rick nothing for Dan Sweder was still very much alive. 'Sounds mysterious! I suppose you know you only wounded Dan Sweder.'

'I suppose you know you gave me a bum cheque?' said Rick sarcastically.

Rex Rand kept his dignity because in truth he had had plenty of experience in passing off such little situations in a life which was alternatively comparatively wealthy and then impecunious.

'Sorry, old man! Truth is my film makers are holding a terrific sum back which should be due to me. I should not have given you the cheque. Truth is. I forgot. However, it doesn't seem to matter.'

'Okay, forget it,' snapped Rick. 'I've got something else in mind. How about you visiting Miss Gloria Grahame — just a nice little friendly visit at her home?'

'I don't think she'd want to see me,' said the other doubtfully. 'I think she's scared of this Sweder guy. Can't be any other reason. No doubt she has gone to him, but I can't see why she should prefer this low swine to me if she wasn't scared of him.'

'She'd see you if you called at her home.'

'Sure,' said Rex Rand. 'Gloria is being foolish, but we are still friends.'

'Okay, get your jalopy out and drive over. Go see the gal. What the hell, she might have changed towards that slob Sweder. You never know with dames.'

'You seem to know,' said the other, and Thelma Wain gave him a bleak glance. 'But what's behind all this? Why should I do this?'

Rick slapped Rand on the arm. 'Hell, man, you're in love. You wanna see the dame, don't you?'

'Sure, but I don't get it.'

'Look, you're going over!' grated Rick Manton. 'Because I say it: Get it now, Mr. Rand? If you don't go, I might get peeved about that bum cheque. I might do something you wouldn't like. I might send some low thug up here to hurt you and you wouldn't like that seeing you're just getting over that first beating up!

147

Okay? You'll go see the dame?'

Rex Rand drew a deep breath. 'All right! Sure! Why not? I was thinking about visiting Gloria again in any case. You needn't threaten me.' All the same the man seemed uneasy. 'Sure, I'll get my car out now and drive over.'

Some minutes later they watched the actor back an auto out of a two-car garage. Maybe the man was hard up for real dough but he had plenty of the properties of life, what with his mock Spanish house and two autos. But maybe everything was in debt!

Rick and Thelma walked down to their auto. The girl said: 'Now what, Perry Mason?'

'Soon as that lug gets going,' explained Rick, 'we get to a phone and call Walt Napier.'

'Walt Napier!'

'Yeah. Baby, you sound like my stooge! If you'd wait until I finish! Yeah, Walt Napier is gonna hand out a report to Dan Sweder about how Rex Rand is having a little talk with the Gloria skin. That way Dan Sweder won't suspect a frame.'

'All right, it's your party,' said Thelma Wain. She thrust slender fingers through her red hair. 'You put it over, m'boy. And for Gawd's sake get this Sweder slob this time!'

They waved to Rex Rand as he set off in a big auto that gleamed and purred and occupied far too much room.

'Okay, let's get to that phone!' snapped Rick Manton.

This task took only seconds, and then Rick Manton dialled a number that he got out of the directory. He was lucky, for he got through to Walt Napier immediately. The man was in his office.

'Look. Napier, this is Rick Manton. I want you to ring Dan Sweder and tell him his dame is entertaining that Rex Rand hero. As a matter of fact, she is — or will be pretty soon because the guy is on his way over.'

There was a little silence. Rick could imagine the wary shamus turning the details over in his mind. Then:

'Why should I do this?'

'Because Sweder hires you to snoop on this dame and you'll be on his good side

149

for this. I've just told you, Rex Rand is on his way over to see the dame.'

'Yeah, I accept that. Why the blazes do you want Dan Sweder to know?'

'Aw, you should worry, Walt! Look, just take it the way it is. Ring Dan Sweder and give him the low-down. That's all. You'll be okay.'

Another appreciable pause as Walt Napier took his time over his decision.

'Okay,' came his voice. 'I gotta hunch about what you're up to. So why should I worry? Sweder hires me to make reports on the dame. So I got one. She's entertaining Rex Rand right now. He'll like that — Sweder, I mean. Why, that guy Rex Rand is courting sudden death!'

'Make the call now,' said Rick urgently. 'Get through to him right away.'

'Yeah. I'll do that.'

'You're safe,' Rick assured the private detective.

There was a chuckle. 'Yeah, I'm safe.' A pause. 'I'll be safer if you succeed in what you want to do!'

Rick Manton heard a click as the man on the other end cradled the instrument.

Rick carne out of the booth, grabbed Thelma's arm and grinned.

'C'mon, we're hitting the road for Sun Avenue again — and I sure hope we have better luck than the last time!'

Very quickly he drove away from Laurel Canyon. He figured there was no chance of catching up with Rex Rand unless the man drove at a snail's pace. Perhaps it didn't matter. But if Rex Rand realised that Dan Sweder, the gangster, was helling up to Sun Avenue he'd have a fit.

When Rick Manton finally approached the Brentwood Park district, after the three-mile trip down Santa Monica Boulevard and turned up Sun Avenue he discovered Rex Rand's auto parked on the concrete driveway of Gloria Grahame's house.

'Well, now, pretty boy has made it,' he remarked. 'Hope he sticks long enough. Not that it really matters as long as Dan Sweder rushes up here. I wouldn't want Rex to get hurt.'

'I suppose he'll be taking her in his arms right now,' murmured Thelma.

'Baby, you sound envious!'

'I am. We're not getting any fun — just this lousy chase after a man we hate.'

'Maybe it won't be long before we're in the money again and having fun together!'

She stirred restlessly by his side.

'Gee, Rick, I hope that will be soon!'

He nodded and drove the hired auto away from Gloria Grahame's house. They had some quick work to accomplish.

He got the auto hidden around a turn of the road. Even if Dan Sweder noticed it, the man would not connect the car with Rick Manton, for the auto was only recently hired. Then Rick and Thelma hurried down to 323 Sun Avenue again. They walked up the driveway, wasting no time because they did not want to be seen. Beside the entrance there were thick bushes, and Rick pulled Thelma into hiding behind these.

'Will Dan Sweder walk this way?' questioned the girl.

'If he wants to catch Rex Rand with his lady-love he'll have to go through that door.'

'Maybe he won't come!'

'Maybe a lotta things, honey. We wait and see.'

'He might send his hoods up first.'

'Sure — if he suspected a trap. Why should he? Remember, Walt Napier has handed him the information.'

'I'm a bit worried,' she confessed.

He turned, held her, smiled into her pretty face. He then kissed fiercely. She clung to him.

Right there, hidden behind a thick bush, waiting deliberately in order to kill a man, they knew they were terribly in love.

Presently Rick withdrew from her arms. He murmured:

'Look, honey, we've got to watch out for Sweder. Wait until I get you some other time, some other place . . . '

'It's a promise, Rick!' she breathed. 'Make it a promise!'

He smiled at her.

'That's an easy promise. Yeah, I promise you, baby.'

He jerked abruptly to a small gap in the bush. An auto engine had sounded on the driveway. There was no mistaking it; this car was coming slowly up the driveway.

The car came to a halt, swinging

around in front of she house. Rick caught sight of the vehicle. Rick's gun was out, held in a grim fist.

But the fist sank slowly while grim disgust etched in Rick's face. His jaw tightened; lips compressed into a firm line. He brought the gun right down.

The car was an open convertible. It wasn't anything that Rick recognised as belonging to Dan Sweder. There were two men in the auto.

One was Dan Sweder. The other was Walt Napier, and he had been doing the driving.

The two men got out of the auto and walked to the entrance door. Rick raised his gun again. But, cursing inaudibly, he could not hit Dan Sweder without risking Walt Napier's life. He did not want that.

Rick heard an angry exclamation from Thelma. The next instant a gun exploded; the smell of powder flashed up Rick's nostrils.

He turned on the girl with an enraged curse. She was holding the Smith & Wesson.

'You little fool! You've spoilt everything!'

Then Rick stared across the driveway again. The two men had vanished. There certainly wasn't a body lying around.

Rick grabbed Thelma Wain, almost shook her. And, crazily, he realised he had been kissing her only moments ago.

'You might have killed Walt Napier! You couldn't pull off that shot! As a matter of fact, you musta missed both those guys!'

'I thought I could get Dan Sweder!' she yelled. 'You were going to let him pass!'

'Sure! I don't want to kill men everywhere on account of that slob! I figured I couldn't hit him. He was covered by Walt Napier. But you — you — well, you've bust up the play all right now!'

'Aw, Rick, I felt suddenly mad! That guy has the devil's own luck.'

He stared sombrely through the gap in the bush.

'Again something went wrong, and I don't mean that crazy shot you snapped off. Why did Dan Sweder bring Walt Napier over with him? Aw, hell, people do the weirdest things.'

'Now he'll know that was another trap!'

Thelma wailed. 'Let's get out of here.'

'No! Oughta be some wacky things going on inside those walls. After all, Rex Rand is there and Dan Sweder will be as sore as a bear with a hot potato. Let's get around to the rear of this joint. Maybe we can see what's going on through the windows.'

'You want me?' asked Thelma plaintively.

He managed a faint grin.

'Aw, honey, c'mon. Sure you balled up the play but what the hell!'

They eased out of cover very cautiously. Rick gripped his gun, Thelma had stuck her weapon back in her handbag. She realised she had been too hasty — so much she had not even hit one of the men! So much for her marksmanship.

She went with Rick. They sidled around the gable end of the house, went through a trellis door. A few more steps and they were near to long, rectangular windows, designed by someone who had never been on a ranch, to admit the maximum of light.

At that moment, nicely timed by a

clever mobster, Dan Sweder opened a door. The man who appeared first was Rex Rand, with Dan Sweder behind him.

The film actor appeared to be suffering a terrific fear. His face was contorted; words trembled on his lips, formlessly.

Rick Manton saw in a flash that Dan Sweder had a gun in the actor's back.

'Keep back!' snapped the gangster. 'And don't try any tricks, Manton. Unless you'd like this decoy of yours to stop a slug in his kidney!'

9

Sweder Escapes

The scene had a frozen feeling for a long, long moment. Actually the time element was about ten seconds. It seemed longer to Rick Manton.

Dan Sweder had guessed right through to the core of the set-up. Admittedly it did not need a genius for that.

'I'm getting out,' said the mobster. 'I could snap a shot at you, Manton, but this is safer. You won't do anything crazy — not with this guy so close to being dead.'

'You got plenty of luck,' admitted Rick.

'I guess I need it, dealing with a smart guy like you!' rasped the other. 'So you got Walt Napier to cross me! You'll find him inside the house, with a cracked skull.'

'You walloped him?'

'What else? He phoned me, told me

158

this actor punk was giving Gloria his lousy attentions, did I want to do anything about it. I did. I thought it would be a good idea to bring Walt Napier up here to scare Rex Rand. The guy doesn't seem to realise who I am. I figured Walt Napier would tell him. I guessed it was a frame the moment that shot nearly took my lid off. What's the matter, punk, you a bad shot or something?'

Rick ignored that.

'You aim to give me your life story?' he sneered. 'Why, if you didn't have a rod in that guy's back — '

'But I have,' interrupted Dan Sweder, 'and I'm going — before the cops tear up here. Folks don't like shots and they got phones.'

'You're so lucid,' sneered Rick. He thought there was just a chance that the other might get enraged and lose his grip on Rex Rand. But there didn't seem much chance. Dan Sweder had a hold on the actor. With Sweder's hurt shoulder, the effort must have been causing him pain. Any guy but Rex Rand could have shaken the gang leader off. But the actor was deeply frightened.

Dan Sweder backed, taking Rex Rand with him. It was a difficult movement, which caused anger to suffuse Dan Sweder's face. Step by step they went down the patio and then through the trellis door. Rick followed warily, his face a leaden mask, with narrowed eyes that watched every movement of the gang leader.

They were on the driveway, still a tense group of people when the thing became an anticlimax.

They were all at once aware of a mailman walking steadily up the driveway to the mailbox on the white post outside the entrance to the house.

The man did not realise be was walking into a strange scene. He smiled and nodded, and then something about the group struck him. The mailman stared.

'Say — ' he began.

All at once Dan Sweder, timing it nicely again, thrust Rex Rand from him and jumped to the convertible. The actor sprawled to the ground. The mailman stared in astonishment. Rick had shoved his gun into his jacket pocket the moment he sighted the mailman.

It was too late and it was certainly the wrong moment to fire at Dan Sweder. The mere presence of the mailman stopped that sort of play.

Dan Sweder, despite a wounded shoulder, got the auto moving. With a jerk and a roar of open throttle, it sprang away. In seconds the set-up dissolved into a group of wary people conscious that the mailman was a guy with many questions.

Rick Manton did not intend to answer any! He turned abruptly, took Thelma's arm and walked around to the rear of the house. Rex Rand, with a spasm of anger now that real danger seemed past, walked unsteadily after them.

'Say, Manton, you sent me up here knowing that swine was coming after me!'

'Aw, shut up!'

'Damn you, Manton, you're a hard devil! You might have got me killed!'

'Would that have been so terrible?' Rick flung back.

'That man is a gangster! Say, why don't

I go to the police?'

'Talk to cops about Dan Sweder and you'll qualify for the morgue darn quick!'

'God! I wonder what I got into — '

'Aw, go to hell!' Thelma yapped at him.

All the same he followed them into the house. They came into a lounge where a Japanese manservant and Gloria Grahame bent over Walt Napier. He was lying on a settee. He wasn't unconscious. He seemed to come out of it as Rick Manton and the others came into the room.

Rick bent over the man.

'You gonna be okay?'

'I sure hope so!' muttered Napier, 'Sweder gave me a nice crack! All on account I crossed him!'

Gloria Grahame squealed: 'Oh, you're just a lot of crooks! Get out of here! What do you think my house is? I'll — I'll — call the police! Get out!'

Rick snarled: 'Shuddup! Your pal, Dan Sweder, is the biggest crook going. You want the cops to finger him?'

There was a babble of voices for some time. Rex Rand figured this was a fine opportunity for him to comfort Gloria.

Walt Napier wanted some explanations, and got them. He wasn't any better off for them. As he explained to Rick: 'I'm on a limb now! I've always kept my nose clean with everybody. Now I double-cross Dan Sweder, of all guys!'

'Look, you won't have to worry about the slob if I can blast him!' hissed Rick Manton.

Walt Napier felt his cranium gingerly.

'I'm worrying now, bud!'

Rick eyed him shrewdly.

'Sure, you're out with Sweder from now on. Soon as he gets to thinking about you, he'll want your hide. Your best bet is to work with us.'

'You expect me to think about that with a cracked skull?' snarled the man.

'Okay, we'll get away from here.'

'You bet, before some cops arrive about that shot. I'm a private detective with a licence to keep. I'm no damned lousy crook.'

'Meaning I am!' grated Rick. 'Okay, okay. So we're not arguing. We're getting away. I wanna talk with you when you can use your brains again.'

'All right. Maybe I'll listen to you. Say, Sweder is lucky! Imagine him bringing me over here to give the actor the works! I didn't dare refuse, although I knew you were planning something — ' He broke off, and have a groan. 'I don't feel so good. Maybe I oughta quit this racket and buy me a farm — if I had anything to buy it with!'

'You private dicks are full of wishful thoughts. Aw let's get outa here.'

Some time later they left the residence on Sun Avenue and walked warily up to Rick's hired car. Rex Rand stayed behind, having some success in comforting Gloria.

Walt Napier sat in the rear seating as Rick drove steadily through the Brentwood Park district. There wasn't any sign of a cop. Maybe the solitary shot had sounded like a backfiring exhaust.

Rick decided to work on Walt Napier's apprehensions.

'Sure, Sweder will hate your guts. He'll figure you knew we were up there ready to blast him.'

'You don't have to draw a blueprint.'

'Okay. Maybe you'd like to help us? We're prepared to take risks to eliminate Sweder. He's cut us out in the dope racket, and everywhere we look we get the brush-off because of this guy.'

'How can I help? I don't want to get mixed up with your murderous plans,' grated Walt Napier.

'Because you're scared,' said Rick coolly. 'You'd kill a guy easily enough except you get scared. Lots of guys can kill — you think about it. Just don't talk like we were dirt. If you can help us that's okay. You got any ideas how we can get Dan Sweder? He's having more luck than old Nick!'

'I got one idea,' said Walt Napier slowly.

Rick flung a sideways glance; then back to the road He was just trickling along. 'Let's have it, feller! Remember, you got a vested interest in eliminating Sweder, and why — because the gink might eliminate you. Chew on that, bud!'

The remarks made Walt Napier's face settle grimly.

'Okay. You're right. And I got something that will interest you. I've told you I

165

don't work for Dan Sweder — just accepted the chore of snooping on the Gloria bitch. But I know plenty about Sweder's rackets. Well, tonight he takes that yacht of his out of the harbour on a special trip. Ain't often the boat goes out. This time it's going to a little island just way round by Santa Catalina Island — a little uninhabited place called Seal Rocks.'

Rick halted the auto carefully, pulling into a curb. He switched off the engine. got out cigarettes and handed them around. 'Okay. Sounds good. Tonight. huh? Ain't that slob having a busy time! What's he want to take the yacht out to Seal Rocks for?'

'It's a party,' explained Walt Napier. 'I got to know all about it. Dan Sweder has invited a number of guys, all of them moneyed dope-takers, to take the trip. Dan will provide gals and drink. The suckers will pay. It's everybody's idea of a swell time. They just hell around. They couldn't care less where the *Green Lady* takes 'em. But the ship will anchor off Seal Rocks for some hours; then return to the L.A. yacht harbour.'

'All that will take the best part of twenty four hours,' observed Rick. 'Wait, it's a cinch! Brother, this is it!'

Thelma Wain was excited. 'Gee, Rick, you could hand that guy everything he's asked for! Out there! There ain't any cops on uninhabited islands!'

Rick dragged hard on his cigarette. 'Let's get the facts sorted out, Walt. Now, are you sure Dan Sweder is going on the yacht — ?'

They spent half-an-hour discussing the set-up. At the end Rick Manton was sombrely satisfied. He figured Dan Sweder's luck could not last. He'd meet his fate, maybe out there on an uninhabited island.

'The set-up couldn't be better,' he stated. 'So we hire another boat. A small, fast cruiser will be okay. We get to Seal Rocks before Sweder's yacht, hide somewhere. After that, who knows?' Rick paused. 'You'll be with us, Walt.'

The other started. 'Me? No. I don't want any part of it,'

'You're in it now,' said Rick grimly. 'You've given us the lowdown. And you oughta know your best guarantee of future living is m the hope that Dan Sweder ain't around anymore.'

Silence hung in the air until words faltered from Walt Napier's lips.

'Okay. You're a smart devil, Manton. You got me in a fix. I'll go with you.'

'That's fine. Because I'd decided you were going in any case. I don't want you trying to get back in Dan's favour by talking to him — maybe over a phone, trying to fix a double-cross!'

The decision was taken. For the rest of the day they based their preparations on the fact that they might have a busy night. First, they visited a yacht yard two miles below Santa Monica and hired a cabin cruiser. Rick told the proprietor he wanted the boat fully fuelled and ready for that night. They were crazy photographers, he explained, and wanted moonlight pictures. The yacht owner said there wouldn't be much moon that night. Rick said the hell with that, they would take pictures anyway.

With Walt Napier, they returned to the trailer high up in the hills and rested and ate. The shamus wasn't too happy. In fact, he spent his time staring morbidly at the cream-coloured wall. His presence was a bit of a nuisance, for Rick Manton suddenly realised the little spell of inactivity was an ideal time to make love to Thelma.

An hour or so passed with little talk. There had been enough of that. Rick checked his gun and then took Thelma's rod and checked that. Walt Napier noticed this work but made no attempt to inspect his own gun.

Rick Manton lay on a settee and dozed. He felt comfortable, and, anyway, he thought they might be up half the night. He'd have felt better with Thelma in his arms.

Thelma Wain lay on the other settee. opposite Rick and thought it a shame she could not lie down with him. She felt drowsy. It was quiet up here in the green hills, and the trailer was warm.

Walt Napier did not even notice her long, slender legs stretched out on the settee. He was thinking.

When Rick Manton swung slowly out

of his sleep, he knew something was wrong. He needed three seconds of reaction to realize the truth.

Walt Napier had vanished!

10

Night Cruise

Walt Napier got a lift down from the hills into central Los Angeles. Motorists were wary of offering lifts to those padding the hoof, but the shamus held his police licence aloft and gained a driver's interest that way.

In town he made for his office and sat down. The evening was thinning into dusk: neons were warming up; a million lights on Broadway and Crenshaw were on, anticipating night. Walt Napier nearly bit his nails in his indecision. Then he reached for his phone.

After the talk to Dan Sweder he rushed out of his office, pausing only long enough to lock the door after him. He went into the street and got a cab.

He wanted to lose himself in central Los Angeles for the next twenty-four hours.

Walt Napier was a very shrewd guy.

Minutes after the phone talk, a sedan braked harshly outside the private detective's office, and two thick-set men jumped out. They went up the stairs and tried the detective's office door.

Then, disgruntled, they returned to the auto, hung around for some time and then drove away.

Walt Napier had been pretty shrewd. He'd thought it was good insurance to talk to Dan Sweder because if Rick Manton failed Dan was the guy to please; and if Rick didn't fail, there was nothing to worry about.

Up in the trailer in the Baldwin Hills, Rick and Thelma debated the private detective's vanishing trick. They were getting ready to drive down to the sea.

'He got scared,' stated Rick. 'Backed out. He's a yellow-belly, anyway.'

'We don't need him, Rick.'

'Nope. I'd just like to know what goes on in his mind. I figure he just got scared. He wanted to get out, so he beat it. And we went to sleep!'

'These trailers are warm.'

'Yeah. Well, we've got work to do. But before we start moving, come here, honey. I made you a promise some time back, and I'm a guy who keeps 'em!'

She went willingly into his arms.

Soon they had to return to practical matters. They locked the trailer and climbed into the auto. As the engine purred them down the gradient, Rick thought maybe this was the last stage of the hell-around. He hoped so because he was becoming sick of chasing a guy for his life. It wasn't anything you got fun out of.

At the yacht harbour they parked the auto in a shed where it was out of sight. The night was indeed rather black, as the yacht proprietor had warned. Rick thought that was all to the good. With the girl, he walked along the pier, came to a cabin where a light gleamed. A moment later he was bandying a few remarks with the owner of the boats.

'Everything ready?'

'Sure. Your ship is riding at the pier and ready. Won't get many moonlight photographs tonight!' The man chuckled.

'We'll use special apparatus,' said Rick quickly.

'Don't see any,' said the man.

'We got it in the auto. Okay, sleep well, Mister.'

And Rick Manton got out of the cabin. He figured the man was too damned observant.

Rick and Thelma walked down to the cabin cruiser and stepped on board. Within a minute Rick was acquainted with the craft. It had car-type controls. He started the motor easily, slipped in a clutch and let the cruiser slide from the pier. He had a chart and a compass, but he thought the best bet was to follow the ferry out of L.A. harbour.

He had figured it out long ago. The ferry went regularly to Catalina Island, and the ferry-boat was unmistakable because of its blaze of lights. Seal Rocks would be located south of Santa Catalina and a bit of compass work would help there.

Minutes later the cruiser was slipping through the choppy water under the impulse of a good motor. Rick and

Thelma sat in the red-leather seat, Rick with his hand lightly on the car-type wheel. As he had nothing to do, he slid one arm around the girl. They were two alone in the night, on the dark Pacific Ocean, the shore already a mile behind.

'The ferry ought to pass pretty soon, if they stick to their darned schedule — and they will,' remarked Rick. 'It might be slow, but we tool along in its wake. According to the time Walt Napier gave us, we'll be a long way ahead of Dan Sweder's yacht.'

'Those lugs don't consider the night has started until they've got some drink under their belts,' observed Thelma.

He smiled, glanced at her in the half-light. The breeze ruffled her hair. He thought her profile was good, perhaps a bit obstinate, wilful, but he liked her the way she was. He leaned forward, his firm lips taking hers and applying pressure. Her lips were soft, willing, tempting — as always!

'You'll be off-course, skipper, if you don't attend to business,' she murmured, breaking away.

He laughed. He throttled the engine back; kept the cruiser barely moving. It was some ten minutes later that he sighted the blaze of light that surely indicated the ferry to Avalon, the township on Santa Catalina Island. He let the craft idle along until the ferry was abreast. They heard music, singing.

They saw folks on the many decks. The flood of light reflected on the dark, heaving sea.

For the next hour they followed the ferryboat. The speed wasn't so slow as he had thought. The low shape of Santa Catalina darkened the horizon; lights indicated the harbour and town of Avalon. Rick got out the chart, started to concentrate.

'Baby, this is where I gotta use my brains. So heaven help us. I've gotta locate Seal Rocks. It's roughly five miles south of Avalon.'

Some time later he was satisfied, and he set a course at full speed. The lights of Santa Catalina Island dropped into the darkness behind them.

For the next twenty-five minutes Rick

Manton concentrated on the boat, compass and chart and with peering into the dark night. Then with a grin of triumph the land he was seeking rose like a purplish hump in the night. He throttled back and went down the coast of the little island, seeking a place to lie in waiting. He found a sandy cove where the sea was comparatively calm. He cut the engine and threw over an anchor and prepared to wait the arrival of the *Green Lady*. Dan Sweder's yacht.

Sitting down for a smoke he observed: 'We gotta little dinghy if we want to get ashore. In fact, we'll need it soon as we know where Dan Sweder intends to anchor and how long he figures to stick around here.'

'Mightn't be long,' replied Thelma. She moved and sat close to Rick. 'I don't get it, coming all the way out here in the night.'

'It's a crazy idea of pleasure. They gotta take the yacht somewhere, and while it's moving they drink, make love and dope. Then hours later they head back and figure they've had a terrific time.'

Thelma went down into the little cabin lit a stove and boiled coffee. With inactivity, they felt the chill in the sea breeze.

An hour after Rick had anchored his craft, the lights of another yacht crept slowly up to Seal Rocks. Rick, of course, spotted them immediately. He watched intently.

'She's still moving slowly, Thelma. Looks like the craft is heading into a bay just around that point.'

Some minutes later the lights of the *Green Lady* had vanished.

Rick Manton knew the craft was around a point of land. The craft was probably very close inshore.

He had the lights snapped off in his own cruiser. He had done that earlier. He started the engine again and allowed the boat to slip out of the bar. Very slowly, because he did not want to ram some rocks, he made a course towards the position where he had last seen the *Green Lady*.

By the time Rick Manton nosed the cruiser around the point Dan Sweder's yacht had anchored. There was a wide bay and an unruffled sea. Rick cut the engine at once. He hardly desired to advertise his presence. He allowed the cruiser to drift and then, still two hundred yards away from the *Green Lady* he flung the anchor overboard again.

'Okay. We'll watch these ginks a moment,' he muttered, 'then maybe we row over in the dinghy, see if we can board the yacht. With that row going on, we should be able to find Dan Sweder and let him have it.'

Sounds of laughter echoed across the waters. A radio was going full-blast. Shrieks of merriment split the night air. Most of the laughter was feminine, except when a coarse bellow came from some guy having the high old time! Rick smiled thinly. The row was all the better from his point of view.

Rick sat close to Thelma; felt the warmth of her. She was desirable. He was in love with the girl. It was the way she talked to him, the way she laughed with him, the softness in her green eyes when she looked at him.

Then he looked grimly across the bay, hearing the riotous merry-making, seeing the blaze of light. There was a guy he wanted to kill. Somehow the whole thing had got in-bitten; he couldn't stop now. It would stop only when Dan Sweder was dead.

Rick Manton never thought that *he* might die.

Finally he stirred from Thelma's close embrace. 'Got to move it, baby. Sorry. I've got to get over to that yacht.'

'You said we would go over!'

'A slip of the tongue, baby, I'm going alone. It just needs one gun. I ain't going to shoot up the whole yacht.'

She had to accept, although she didn't like it.

He got the dinghy ready. He lowered it to the water without a splash. From the amount of row emanating from the *Green Lady* it wouldn't have mattered how much noise Rick Manton made.

He pushed off from the cruiser and used the paddles silently; he thought he saw Thelma as a shadow. Then the next time he looked back she was not there.

There wasn't even the outline of the cruiser. He felt very lonely in the small boat. He was disconnected from Thelma and the bright lights and row of the *Green Lady*. He had a fanciful idea that he was dreaming all this.

Then, when he got close to the big yacht, he discarded these fantastic notions. Soon he was near enough to reach out and touch the side of the ship. He shoved the dinghy around until it was close to a gangway that ran down the side of the yacht. Rick Manton tied the dinghy to the gangway. He figured he wanted the little boat for the return trip.

Then, gun in hand, he went up the gangway. He crept on to the deck, grinned at the row and stepped forward a pace.

At that moment figures hurtled at him from all sides. Men sprang like determined foes from all manner of hiding places.

It suddenly screamed at Rick Manton that he had walked into a complete trap!

11

Kill-Feast

Rick blasted with his gun before sheer weight bore down on him. He heard a man yell in agony. Then hands were clutching at him, his gun fell to the deck. He clawed out of savage hands; jerked back to the rail.

Rick Manton became a vicious fighting animal. He hacked with fists and kicked. He felt his right and then his left scrape stubbly chins. His foot nearly disemboweled a man.

Rick knew immediately he couldn't win. He could not beat four or five men. So he had to escape, but fast. So far they had not got a real grip on him.

He jerked back, left half his jacket in a man's hands. He had a wild thought to the effect that it was a good thing he had left the best part of his dough in the trailer before setting out. Then he was hard against the yacht rail. The tube rammed in his back. He knew the sea was below him. He thought the sea was better than these guys. He kicked again; heard a man hack for breath. It was like a siren with asthma. Then Rick slammed one man back against another.

There was about half-a-second of respite. The man who can leap over a rail in half-a-second is good. Rick Manton did it. His leap was a tigerish spring: muscles reflexing like the wild brute itself.

He hit the water in an ungainly sprawl. He went down deep. He kicked out and swam away from the yacht, keeping submerged for as long as possible. Then he surfaced, grabbed a lungful of air and swam madly for the shore.

As he had anticipated, a shot rang out, but the slug was wide of him. He plunged on, realising the shore was the safest place and the quickest to gain. Another shot cracked the night. Dan's hoods were having target practice, but they were not hitting the bull.

Rick heard the sound of a boat being

lowered. He knew he had not a chance to swim all the way back to the cabin cruiser. They would pick him up before he got halfway. He had to reach the shore and dive into the darkness of the island.

He had lost his gun, and for the moment he could not return to Thelma on the cruiser. He thought the cruiser was far enough away to escape notice in the dark night. But what if Dan Sweder's hands had a searchlight?

Rick felt the beach under his feet, He scrambled up and disappeared into a tangled undergrowth of stunted trees and bushes. He had an impression of shouts ringing out from the *Green Lady*. Somebody was plenty mad that he had gotten away.

Rick Manton gritted his teeth when he realised the hoods had been waiting for him. So Dan Sweder had known Rick Manton would turn up! But how?

Then Rick knew. Even as he thrust through the tangled bushes, he realised that Walt Napier had talked. No one else had known about the plan to follow Dan Sweder to Seal Rocks. So it had to be

Walt Napier. Any moron could figure that one out.

Right then and there it didn't make any difference who had done what. He was in a jam. He had lost his gun, he was on some lousy island and there were several hoodlums ready to come after him. What was worse there was danger that the cruiser and Thelma might be discovered. Obviously Dan Sweder would know there was another boat somewhere around.

Rick Manton halted, gasped for breath and listened for sounds of pursuit. He heard nothing except his own harsh breathing and the sigh of leaves and branches around him. Seemed he had outdistanced his pursuers.

But that wasn't so good except for momentary benefit. If Dan Sweder's hustlers located Thelma, they could sail away and leave him stranded on this lousy island. As it was uninhabited and seldom visited, that was a pretty set-up!

He made a swift guess as to the position of the sea, and then he thrust forward again, carefully, grimly. The best thing to do in the circumstances was to get back on board the cruiser and figure out some different plan.

Rick Manton pushed through clinging bushes and some variety of thorn that made him curse. This was good! He was like some darned hick up in the mountains! He was a city guy. He didn't like this way-back stuff.

Eventually he came to a portion of the beach where a few palms grew close to the sea. He used them as cover. He stared across the sea. He couldn't see Dan Sweder's yacht. Apparently he had cut across the island and there was now a point of land between him and the vessel's lights.

Rick still retained his sense of direction. Even if he was a city-bred man he had plenty of that. He set off along the beach grimly apprehensive. There was plenty of cover for him but it might operate two ways. He'd never know until the last moment when he might run into some of Dan Sweder's hoods.

All the same he had to get back to the cruiser. Thelma would have heard the shots and be in an agony of mind. She might do something crazy.

Rick tramped on, and then, finding the beach was deserted he began to run. He climbed some rocks, gradually got around the point of land. Suddenly he saw the distant lights of the *Green Lady*. Then he knew his cabin cruiser was just off this part of the shore. He couldn't see the vessel. But it must be somewhere out there in the darkness.

He waded into the sea. He stared into the night, trying desperately to pierce the gloom. He thought he saw the shape of the cruiser out there in the night, but he wasn't sure. He had to be sure. He had to get on board that craft, show Thelma he was okay. She'd be dying of anxiety!

He felt sure the boat was lying out there in the night. He plunged into the sea; struck out with a vigorous stroke. He swam grimly for some minutes, then raised his head. Still he could not see the cruiser. Despairingly he thought the damned craft had to be there. Thelma was there, out in the night.. Thelma . . . real and solid . . . familiar!

He swam on doggedly. It was years

since he had done so much, although he had been pretty good when at high school. He began to tire. Treading water he raised himself, stared savagely at the bland face of night.

He could not see the cabin cruiser anywhere!

He twisted: saw the distant lights of Dan Sweder's yacht. He cursed the gangleader. He struck out blindly; thought he ought to get back to shore. He couldn't find Thelma — couldn't find her . . . find her . . . find her . . . He began to whimper. He was out of his element.

He twisted around, struck out blindly for the beach of the little island. He was tired; had swallowed too much water. He got the desperate feeling that he'd never make it.

And then, in the night, he heard the dull thud of something hitting wood. He jerked around, stared through water and the night.

He saw the shape. The shape of a boat. The cabin cruiser!

It wasn't really far away. It was rocking idly on the sea. He heard the shuffling sound again and knew it for footfalls on wooden deck.

He flung forward in a wild swim. He threshed the water, sliced through it with grim fury. Then he shouted:

'Thelma! It's me — Rick!'

A few more savage strokes which disregarded the fact that his arms were fashioned from lumps of lead, and he was alongside the cruiser. He hauled himself up; got a leg over the side.

A hand reached out; hauled him up.

Rick suddenly knew it was a man's hand. Despair twanged through taut nerves. With something like a sob he twisted free; shoved hands up in an uncertain guard.

A man rammed a fist to his chin. Rick Manton staggered back, halted because he hit a bulkhead. Rick hacked horribly for breath, spat and thrust fresh, desperate strength into his limbs.

The attacker was stupidly slow. He gave Rick valuable seconds. When he came across the deck, Rick Manton recognized him as Zac Ortmann. One flashing glance through the dark was enough. Rick sucked and rasped for more breath and then, savagely, recklessly flung himself at the man.

Zac Ortmann was a city-bred hood. He could roughhouse but he was happier in a barroom sneering at someone who wasn't able to do a thing about it. Even so, he had plenty of advantages at that moment over Rick Manton. Rick was dead-beat. Rick had swam a good distance, fought off some other men, run across an island.

But Rick Manton wasn't going under to some lousy hoodlum. Thinking about what had happened to Thelma simply crazed him. He scooped savagely at the other's face. His fist connected in a blow that rasped downwards. It was like ploughing rocky earth with the bare fists. Zac Ortmann did not like it. He emitted a snarling cry; then hunched as if to get protection for another flashing fist. Then with bunched shoulders, he tried to ram Rick Manton. Rick hung on to the man as they went backwards. Rick slammed another at Zac Ortmann. The man's head jerked back. Rick wanted to keep the man's head up. He slammed away intensely, blindly. Zac Ortmann could not stand much of the treatment. After three, four blows he wobbled, tried automatically to back away. But his legs apparently got a delayed action from his buffeted head, and he sagged down to the deck. He was on his knees when Rick planted the finishing blows. Then he rolled over, unconscious.

Rick Manton frisked the man. Rick sobbed for breath, but did not let it stop him working. He got a gun off the man. He figured it was loaded; he did not check. He thrust it into his pocket. Then, picking up Zac Ortmann bodily, he advanced to the rail with clenched teeth.

In a moment the hoodlum went over the side. The sea took him with hardly a murmur.

'That's you, blast you!' sobbed Rick, 'The end of you!'

He turned, dived down into the cabin.

A few seconds later he knew Thelma was not on the small cruiser. Zac Ortmann had been the only person!

What had happened to the girl? Was she alive?

Rick Manton went to the side and stared over the brooding sea. He didn't want to think about it. He couldn't think that the sea had received Thelma as well as the vicious Zac Ortmann.

But it could have happened. Dan Sweder or his men had been on the cruiser. Unless they had taken Thelma away to the *Green Lady* she —

Rick turned away, a cold, dead feeling in his guts. He put his hand in his remaining pocket, felt the gun. He probably looked a wreck. He felt terrible. Because if Thelma was dead, he'd be dead except that he'd go on living long enough to take some other guys to the graveyard!

The graveyard. Maybe that was the end for them all. And maybe it wouldn't take fifty years to get there, either! Maybe the end wasn't so far away. Was death all round to be the result of this kill-feast?

He didn't know. He approached the controls, switched on the engine. He stamped on the starter; the works chugged into life. He let in the clutch and the craft began to glide.

Naturally he was going to locate Dan Sweder, discover what had happened to Thelma and then kill him.

And Dan Sweder was probably on his yacht. It seemed that the unlucky Zac Ortmann had been left in charge of the cruiser.

Rick Manton sent the cruiser forward across the bay in a swift glide and then, when there was plenty of momentum, he cut the engine again. Although the *Green Lady* was still a blaze of light and productive of sounds of raucous merriment, he hardly wanted to be noticed. Maybe Dan Sweder was on the island with his hoods, looking for the man he hated. Maybe not. That remained to be discovered.

A blaze of red light was flaring on the island. The merry-makers had started a bonfire. As Rick glided in closer, he saw groups of people around the bonfire and heard giggles and guffaws. It seemed the pleasure-bent section of the party knew nothing of the grimmer side of the trip. Judging by the row, they were too drunk to understand anything.

Rick Manton let the cruiser drift slowly up to the *Green Lady*. He had the gun in one hand. He wasn't going to attempt any more swimming. He wanted the gun kept nice and dry! He felt a wreck. He was a battered devil in torn clothes, and he'd probably frighten anybody on a dark night — except Dan Sweder or his hoodlums! He wasn't thinking about scaring Dan Sweder; just wanted to kill him.

The cruiser lightly touched the yacht. Rick used his hands to thrust the craft along until it was close to the gangway. When he saw the dinghy still tied up, he smiled ironically. He whipped a mooring rope from the cruiser to the gangway. Then, gun in hand, he went up the steps.

Sure as Hades he wasn't going to be taken by surprise this time. He'd shoot. He reckoned he could take six men. He hoped one would be Dan Sweder.

On the deck he paused momentarily. There wasn't anyone in sight; and then he heard foolish voices and footsteps. A man and a woman turned a corner bulkhead, swaying and laughing, arms around each other.

Rick Manton grinned thinly; tried an experiment. He walked past the couple, said, 'Good night!'

'Good night, ol' boy!' slurred the man. 'Beautiful!' cooed the blonde.

Rick Manton went on. He thought the pair must have been tight as weiner skins. They'd noticed nothing unusual about him. They thought he was one of the party. That was a good point. With so many folks around, all drunks, he stood a good chance of escaping detection.

Thoughts of Thelma urged him on. He had to find out what had happened to her. He slid down a companionway, went along a passage towards the cabins. He just had to look around. He had to start somewhere.

He looked in one cabin, saw it was empty. He was about to back out when he caught sight of the clothes lying untidily on a bunk. He saw blue serge trousers, jacket and a peaked cap. Rick dived into the cabin, pulled the door shut. He ripped off his own torn clothes. He got into the new duds and pulled the peaked cap down over his eyes. He stuffed his old things away out of sight under the bunk. He even managed a grin. Now he might look like one of the crew in the semi-dark.

He went out into the corridor again. Within seconds he was beside a door that was open an inch. Beyond was the gaming room and some male diehards were still playing poker, apparently for high stakes. Rick's eyelids flickered grimly. Any other time he'd have chanced walking in and cleaning these guys out of their dough!

But not now. He withdrew and moved along down the corridor. Right inside Rick Manton's hard, grim soul something was crying out: 'Thelma! Thelma! God, kid, I've got to find you!'

His gun felt like a cannon. It was waist-high all the time, prominent. He moved along, paused beside another cabin door. He listened. As he was listening a man staggered out of a stateroom. Rick's gun went down by his side quickly. The guy walked past, giving a stupid, drunken wave of his hand.

Rick Manton walked on, slid back a door savagely. The cabin beyond was in darkness. He fumbled for a light switch. He couldn't find it. Cursing, he was about to withdraw. Then he heard a kicking sound.

He did get the switch. Light flooded the small cabin. With sheer incredulity slowing him he saw the bound figure of a girl lying on a bunk. It was Thelma!

He never knew he made the steps towards her; hardly realised how he got the bindings from her. But the next moment she was in his arms. She was crying, violent sobs of reaction. Then, harshly, she checked them. She was that kind of a girl.

'You made a sound . . . to attract me . . . in the dark?' he questioned.

'I knew it was you, Rick! I just knew. Don't ask me how! Aw, God, Rick, let's get away! I'm sick of the whole thing! I — I — thought you were dead!'

12

Pay Back

He grated: 'Jeeze, and I thought you were dead! And then I thought you couldn't be . . . not you . . . Thelma . . . not you . . . dead!'

'I heard the shooting. Then they rowed over and got me.'

'Didn't you use your gun?'

'Yeah, but it was dark and they waited until they had two boats — one on each side of the cruiser.'

'Aw, the hell with them, anyway! Let's get outa here. I've killed Zac Ortmann and got the cruiser back. Let's move it baby.'

She had not been tied long and there was nothing to stop her moving vigorously, which she did. They walked swiftly along the corridor. Without opposition, they went up to the deck.

It was on the deck that they were practically roped into a party! A group were dancing drunkenly and singing. A man caught hold of Thelma and swung her into a circle. Rick started forward with a curse but was halted by a man who handed him a bottle.

'Have a drink wi' me, pal!'

Rick tried to get Thelma out of the circle, but the whole party began to swirl in a crazy dance. The men holding Thelma had a tight grip. Rick Manton was grabbed by two women who must have been out of the chorus, because they had muscles. For some minutes Rick and Thelma were forced into the crazy merry-making. Then, when Rick Manton did break away he found himself holding the bottle of whisky. He grabbed at Thelma.

'C'mon, we gotta get out of this.'

A few yards away he paused. He eyed the bottle grimly.

'Might as well have a drink, honey. We're about the only persons on this yacht who really need it.'

They drank the bottle between them. He thought this was a crazy scene; a guy with a gun in one hand and a bottle of whisky in the other, on this goddam yacht, with drunks all around, and

Thelma by his side. And there, nearly at the sea-edge, was a huge bonfire sending sparks and a red flare into the sky. People were circled around it, although the night was hardly cold. And those suckers couldn't be cold, not with all the booze they'd consumed.

And then Rick Manton became rigid. Looking over the rail at the fire he saw three men in a group. Two of them were carrying rifles. They talked, but constantly looked around at the dark shadows beyond the bonfire.

Rick recognised one of the men as Dan Sweder.

Maybe it was the drink he had just swallowed, but maybe it was just the return of the hatred he had for this man; whatever the cause he felt a terrible urge to go after the guy and kill him.

Rick raised his gun. Then he lowered it. He knew the range was too much for an automatic. He could not guarantee accuracy at that distance.

Thelma noticed the movement. Then she glanced at the fire, following Rick's fixed, burning gaze.

'Dan Sweder!'

'Yeah. I'm gonna get him.'

'Oh, Rick, don't try it! Rick, I'm sick of this awful play. Let's get down to the cruiser and get away while we have the chance.'

'Why pass this up? I could get that guy! Isn't that what all this is about?'

'But you might get killed!'

He uttered a curt laugh. 'Nuts! That guy ain't killed me yet. And I've eliminated some of his pals. Why should he be so lucky?'

'Don't go, Rick!' she breathed. 'I gotta bad feeling about this!' But he had shaken off her hand. He turned.

'Let's take the dinghy to the shore. You're going with me this time.' Reluctantly she gave in. One thing, she was not going to leave him again. So if he wanted to do this thing it would have to be together.

They climbed down the gangway and got into the little dinghy. He pushed off and then used the paddles. He took the boat around the yacht and headed to a distant part of the island. He certainly did not figure on landing close to the red glare of the bonfire and those men with the rifles.

Rick Manton beached the boat and then dragged up a couple of yards. Thelma stepped on to the beach, looked around half-fearfully. He noticed that. 'Say, baby you ain't losing that nerve, are you?'

'Would you blame me, Rick?'

'Aw, no. Quit worrying. We're not behind the eight-ball. That's where Sweder is.'

Fifty yards down the beach the bonfire flared and created eerie shadows. The pleasure-seekers were still singing and dancing and wandering around. But the three other men stood in a cautious bunch. They were outlined against the red fire. To Rick Manton they made a good target — if he could approach nearer. He thought they were suckers to stand close to the fire.

He could see them clearly, but if he kept in the dark he'd he a bad target.

Rick and Thelma ran up to the fringe of bushes and stunted trees. Then they crept along warily, getting closer to the bonfire, but keeping in the deep gloom. Then a point was reached where Rick Manton paused. His face close to the girl's, he muttered: 'Maybe it's better you go no further.'

'But, Rick, you said we'd go together!'

'Yeah, I know. But when I start shooting there'll only be seconds for a getaway. We gotta get back to the dinghy and push off; get to the cruiser in the confusion and beat it. I guess I'll have to drop those two ginks with the rifles or they'll get us while we're rowing away.'

Her mouth was dry. She could hardly speak. So she brushed her lips on his face and nodded.

'Okay. Stick here. Watch out. When you hear shooting run back to the dinghy and have it ready in the water.'

Then he crept silently away and was lost in the darkness.

Rick Manton used the stunted trees and bushes as cover. The little noise he did make meant nothing. The yelling and singing that emanated from the party around the bonfire was worthy of an Indian war party. Dan Sweder and his rifle-equipped toughies were not exactly helped by the drunks. Probably Dan Sweder figured Rick Manton was still on the island as a fugitive. This was not quite accurate.

Rick became careful as he neared the men standing close to the fire. He could have halted anywhere and chanced some shots. But he hardly wanted risky shooting. He wanted to drop the men immediately. Especially Dan Sweder. It burned in him that the man had manhandled Thelma; would kill her if he got the chance.

Rick came a step closer, and then another. He hugged a bent tree bole. There was a bush a yard ahead. It would afford ideal cover, He was still in the dark. Those suckers were outlined by the red glare behind them. With six shots in his gun he could drop them, given the element of surprise.

Rick made it to the next bush and then settled down to take aim. He knew he could get no nearer. In any case the range was short enough.

Dan Sweder's lean, wiry figure was the

first in his sights. Rick thought somberly: this is it, you slob! You asked for it . . . It's been you or me! Kill or be killed. You wouldn't give a hoot in hell for me if you had the bead on me!

He took time over his aim. He had a problem. Should he take Dan Sweder first or should he drop one of the gunnies with the rifles? He thought Sweder came first.

He was close enough to see the sour impression planted on Dan Sweder's face. The guy was probably mean as hell.

Rick tightened his pressure on his trigger. It would be Dan Sweder first . . . after all . . .

Then something prompted Rick to call out: 'Sweder! You got it coming to you! This is Rick Manton.' Somehow he felt he had to give the other the warning. He wasn't triumphant. He just felt the man was entitled to a warning.

Rick Manton fired as the riflemen snapped crashing shots off into the darkness. The cracking gunshots built up an impression of confusion. Rick did not flinch back. He saw Dan Sweder fall backwards under the impact of the slug.

Then Rick was triggering again. The sound of his own gun was only incidental to the crash of the rifles. Shells whined all around him, hissed and cut the night air.

He got the first gunny with the second shot. The man just folded. The crazy pleasure-seekers were backing in confusion from the bonfire. Rick aimed grimly at the other man with the rifle.

Then, a bullet dug into his chest and spun him around. A burning pain jabbed from the centre of the wound. His left arm hung limply. He had been hit.

Rick stumbled backwards, almost fell. He knew suddenly he had to get away. He was too agonized to aim properly.

He couldn't get the other hood with the rifle.

He thrust into a run that sent pain through him. He stumbled on, thought he heard sounds of pursuit behind him. There was terror in the thought that the rifleman might shoot him in the back. One thing, the night was a friend!

The stumbling run back to the point on the beach where Thelma had the dinghy was a nightmare. She noticed his limp arm. 'You've been hit!'

No more words. They piled into the small boat and pushed it off. He tried to use a paddle one-handed, but it slipped from his grasp, Thelma was using the other desperately. Gradually they were withdrawing from Seal Rocks. Fighting the pain, Rick Manton was in a dazed nausea. He had no idea when or how they reached the cruiser. But they did. They were right under the very bows of Dan Sweder's yacht. Somehow it meant nothing, for Rick was very sure Dan Sweder was no more.

They got aboard the cruiser. Thelma hoisted and dragged the dinghy up. Rick cast off and started the engine. He heard two widely separate shots from the island and judged that the guard with the rifle was potting at shadows.

Their craft guided away from the *Green Lady*. When next Rick looked back, they were an incredible distance from the island and the yacht. The red flare of the bonfire still showed and the lights of the yacht. He heard shouts and some wild singing from some revellers still oblivious to the night's events.

And then Rick Manton turned his head to the wall of night and slowly toppled from his seat.

'Rick!' Thelma screamed. Dropping to her knees, she put her arms under him, tried to raise him to a sitting position. She felt a warm clamminess and instinctively withdrew her arms. Rick sank to the floor. He lay flat on his back, eyes closed.

Thelma looked at her hands. They were thick with blood. She leaned over him. thrust her face close to his.

'Rick! Speak to me! You can't die! *You can't!*'

His eyes flickered open. Hope flared in Thelma's heart. She spoke chokingly:

'Rick, we're going to make a fresh start! This sort of life is no good!'

Rick smiled glassily. 'You — you said it. baby . . . I guess that's why I'm checking out.'

'No! *No!* You're going to be okay! I'll get you to a doctor — '

'No good . . . I'm finished, Thelma. Serves me right . . . I've lived a rotten life . . . death and hate . . . bad all the way. I lived by the gun, and now I'm . . . '

'No! You're *not* dying! You can't leave me — I can't live without you! We'll go to Dallas — give up crime and make a new life! We — '

She broke off as Rick gave an audible sigh. His head rolled gently to one side, became still.

The girl sobbed, flung herself on his lifeless body. She felt the hard outline of the gun in his pocket, poking into her. She reared back as if electrified.

An overwhelming feeling of shame and remorse washed through her veins like acid as Rick's last words reverberated through her skull. He had been right! Their life together had been something rotten. But she knew she could not live without him. However, perhaps there was still a way for them to be together.

With trembling hands she reached for his gun . . .

★　★　★

When the coastguard caught up with the drifting cruiser the next day, there was no one living on board.

We do hope that you have enjoyed reading this large print book.

Did you know that all of our titles are available for purchase?

We publish a wide range of high quality large print books including:
Romances, Mysteries, Classics
General Fiction
Non Fiction and Westerns

Special interest titles available in large print are:
The Little Oxford Dictionary
Music Book, Song Book
Hymn Book, Service Book

Also available from us courtesy of Oxford University Press:
Young Readers' Dictionary
(large print edition)
Young Readers' Thesaurus
(large print edition)

For further information or a free brochure, please contact us at:
Ulverscroft Large Print Books Ltd.,
The Green, Bradgate Road, Anstey,
Leicester, LE7 7FU, England.
Tel: (00 44) **0116 236 4325**
Fax: (00 44) **0116 234 0205**